Endorsements

Autumn Awakening is the sort of book you pick up, thinking it could be an interesting read... and then you simply cannot put it down!

What starts out a cute, somewhat bittersweet family drama - soon turns and twists into a fast paced, fantasy thrill ride with monsters and vampires and ghosts all over the place!

This is not a book you want to miss!

~ JC Morrows, author of the bestselling YA series: Order of the Moonstone

So, I'm reading this book. Everything is going along just fine - and then I'm crying. Can't stop. Don't really want to.

I'm stuck. In Shadowhill. With no plans to ever leave.

Even with all of the bad guys - I don't wanna leave. I want to stay. Read more.

~ Amazon Reviewer

All. The. FEELS!!!

This book is both an emotional roller coaster and a dizzying drop from a tower of terror!

Heart pounding and heartbreaking!

FIVE STARS!

~ Goodreads Reviewer

Books by Macy

Autumn Awakening

Written with JC Morrows

The Alien's Daughter
The Hybrid Challenge

Cindy's Demanding Day
A Challenge for Maree
Rissa's Secret Weapon

AUTUMN *awakening*

AUTUMN *awakening*

in this family...you inherit more than a house

MACY MORROWS

MYSTIC PRESS

For my mom, who always encouraged me

CONTENTS

"SURELY THE LORD GOD WILL DO NOTHING, BUT HE REVEALETH HIS SECRET UNTO HIS SERVANTS THE PROPHETS."

~ Amos 3:7 KJV

AUTUMN *awakening*

WHO AM I

Things I used to worry about on a daily basis...

How my hair looked. Was my nail polish "in"? What was the hottest new thing? Which party would my best friend drag me to this time? Pop quizzes—a health or history test? The latest gossip buzzing about in school.

After a long day I would come home expecting to find my quirky sister's nose in a book and my little brother jumping around, waiting to bug me about the latest video game. That life was simple... I had a best friend, I was on a level just below the "in crowd." I had two parents who loved me, grandparents who adored me.

But my life is no longer simple.

Things I worry about now… What time is sunset? Do I have plenty of pointy wood in my possession? Is this person trustworthy? Will I find a new enemy I have to fight waiting around the next corner? Am I gonna survive this fight? Is my sister gonna be killed by something horrible? Is my mom gonna find out my secret? Who can I trust?

Secrets. Blood. Wood. Death.

Ladies and gentlemen, this is my life. I live and breathe these things. I wish my life could be as simple as the people who don't have a clue. They go about their lives, and they have no idea what's really going on. Right under their noses. Right outside their doors. There has to be someone chosen—and that's me.

I was chosen.

I have no idea who they are—or why they chose me. Maybe there's just something in my blood that awakens to the danger no one else sees.

My name is Hannah Autumn... and this is my life.

LEAVING HOME

September 13th 2018

Hannah sat on her air mattress, staring at her bedroom floor. In her lap, sat her Swiss Shepherd, resting her head. Hannah gently stroked the dog's white, silky fur with her fingers.

Hannah remembered very clearly the day she'd found her dog. It was definitely a happy memory.

She and her mother had seen a flyer for the shelter that said they urgently needed people to adopt animals. So, they'd stopped by for a visit, not really sure they wanted a pet. But when they'd spotted the dog, they both knew she was the one for them.

Someone from the shelter was calling her Freckles, but when Hannah saw her, she knew that was not her name. She named the dog Pumpkin for the tiny spot of orange on her tail. It wasn't dirt. Hannah and her mom had washed Pumpkin thoroughly to make sure it wasn't.

Hannah looked around her room as her fingers stroked Pumpkin's fur. It was pretty much empty. All that remained was the air mattress she was sitting on, a couple of boxes, and a guitar that was leaning up against the wall.

The gloomy blue color on Hannah's bare walls fit her mood perfectly. Her mood had been down since her mother had given her the news about the divorce. It had been months now, and her emotions had only gotten darker... gloomier... in the time they had gone through the business of getting divorced.

Somewhere in the middle of it all, her best friend had stopped talking to her—and her grandfather had died just two months ago. Hannah had been very close to her grandfather. Aside from non-family friends, her grandfather had been her best friend.

Now he was gone.

At the sound of a knock at her door, Hannah slowly looked up. "Come in."

The door opened and Hannah's mother leaned in a little, her hand on the knob as she looked at her daughter, sitting on the air mattress with Pumpkin lying across her lap.

"Hey honey," her mom's voice quiet, her tone soft.

Martha Autumn was wearing brown sandals with three-inch heels, a pair of slightly faded denim jeans, a light blue tee shirt and a plaid jacket with yellow lines crossing blue ones. Her dark, blonde hair was braided, with the braid dangling over her right shoulder.

Hannah, still in mourning for her grandfather, was wearing all dark clothes. She wore her black tennis shoes, dark blue jeans, a dark green top and a black jacket to keep her warm in the fall Manhattan breeze. Her medium blonde hair hung loose over her shoulders.

"It's time to go." Martha told her.

Hannah looked down at the dog on her lap. She knelt down and carefully fastened Pumpkin's leash to her collar as her mother turned on the pump that would deflate the air mattress. Hannah moved over to help her mother, slowly pushing the air out of the little pockets.

When they had managed to empty it as much as possible, they worked together to fold it up and put it in its box.

Hannah walked to the far corner of the room and picked up her guitar case. After placing her guitar gently in the case and fastening the locks, she picked up the case, along with her duffle bag, then she tucked her purse under her arm. Her mom had picked up the box that held the air mattress and was waiting on her. Hannah wrapped the loop on the end of Pumpkin's leash around her wrist, then they headed for the door.

When she was almost to the doorway, the sight of the shiny, new door knob reminded her of the day of her grandfather's funeral. Her family had just come back from the service and Hannah had escaped to her room—wanting to be alone, wanting her grandfather to be alive, wanting to somehow turn back time and find a way to change so many things.

So much anger and sadness and mourning had been churning inside of her—and it had all somehow come out through her when she'd reached to open her bedroom door. She didn't have any other explanation for what had happened.

She had taken hold of the door knob to turn it and open her door. Instead, the metal had crumpled like tissue paper and then crumbled in her hand, leaving nothing to actually open the door—only a tiny, mangled piece of metal that looked similar to the metal shards and dust that lay in her hand.

A shudder rippled over her at the memory—and she squared her shoulders, determined to put it out of her mind. Nothing like that had happened since. And she was set on keeping it that way. She looked away from the shiny knob and took another step, but before she could move past the doorway, she stopped one last time and looked back into the room that had been her sanctuary for three years.

Within these walls, she could see moments that had happened within the walls; times that she and her former friend, Maggie Morris, had played together, afternoons sitting on her bed talking about silly things, trading stories about other kids in their class... this had mostly been Maggie, the times when she had given Hannah a makeover—trying to make them both look more grown up than they were.

There were so many moments.

One of her favorites would always be the time she and her grandfather had played chess on her bed, laughing when too quick a movement would send the pieces toppling out of place.

A tear slid down Hannah's cheek with the picture that formed in her head. There was a tightening in her throat that told her more tears were on their way.

"Honey," her mother's voice was quiet, but Hannah knew from the tone that she could not put her off much longer.

With a sigh and a tiny sniff, she turned around—and a moment later, when her mother gently wiped away the tear that had started to slide down her cheek, she struggled not to stiffen and pull away.

After a second, Hannah's mother let her hand drop. They stood there in the hall for several very long moments, neither one saying anything. Then her mother stepped back, and turned to walk down the hall toward the living room.

"Maggie's downstairs, by the way." Her voice was full of hope, but also caution.

Hannah wanted to snap, but stopped herself. Why would Maggie be here? What could she want? Nothing came to mind, so Hannah decided she would just have to ask. "Why is *she* here?"

"She's waiting to say goodbye." There was surprise in her mother's voice now, which puzzled Hannah. Her mother knew what had happened with Maggie. They were leaving. Why would she want them to make up now?

Still, there was no use in arguing, so she turned and followed her mother down the hall.

Hannah and her mom left the apartment, turning to walk down the hall until they reached the small elevator they had used nearly every day for the past three years.

Martha pushed the button to call for the elevator.

When the door opened, Hannah followed her mother into the elevator, leaning against the back wall as the doors closed. They stood in silence as the floors clicked away, not saying a word until the bell rang, announcing they had reached the ground floor. They walked out of the elevator together and into the lobby.

There wasn't much to the lobby. The front desk was off to the left side of the room. There was usually someone sitting behind the tall counter that was the front of the desk. At the moment, it was empty. The doorman must be off somewhere, tending to some problem or other. The large windows on both sides of the front door were decorated with tall, leafy plants. More plants and chairs sat against the wall across from the front desk.

If you went down the hall on either side of the elevator, you would find a small room with vending machines. Next was an exercise room. The board had once discussed putting in an indoor pool, but they were concerned that it would give outsiders the idea that they could just walk in and use the pool. In the end, they'd decided against it. So despite Hannah and her family's excitement, they did not get their pool.

"You'll like the house, Hannah." Martha said, trying to get Hannah to talk to her.

When that didn't work, she tried another tack. "I know you don't want to see Maggie, but at least talk to her, please. It's not likely you'll see her again, especially after what happened." Martha added, her tone sad. "You used to be friends."

When Hannah still said nothing, Martha went on. "It seems like she wants to make up. Maybe she's sorry." Her mom tried to sound hopeful, but after what they all had been through, she didn't press. She just wanted her daughter's last memories of Maggie to be happy.

"I just don't know what to say anymore, Mom." Hannah's voice was filled with sadness and devoid of any hope as they walked over to the desk. Since no one was at the desk, they had to wait to turn in their keys.

Hannah stared off into space, her face purposely blank. Inside, behind the wall where she kept her heart, Hannah was screaming. From the pain... from the emptiness... from the loss of so many things she held dear... her grandfather, her father, her home, her life, her best friend.

There was just too much.

After a minute, they set down the last of their boxes. Martha looked over at Hannah. She couldn't help feeling sad for her sweet daughter. As a mother, she couldn't stand it when one of her kids was hurting.

All of it made Martha want to smack Maggie for hurting Hannah, but she didn't, not only because she was not Maggie's mother, but because she didn't want to influence Hannah's little brother Ryan, with more violence than what he already had in his young mind.

"You know you can say anything to me, honey." Martha turned to Hannah, and put her left elbow on the top of the counter.

With her right hand, she reached up to Hannah's back and rubbed gently. All Martha really wanted was to get Hannah to talk to her, and then she wanted to find Maggie's parents and teach them a couple of things about discipline and manners.

"I don't want to talk to Maggie." Hannah said.

She gritted her teeth for a second, but then pushed the

anger down into her chest and behind the wall in front of her heart.

"I know, honey." Martha sounded defeated, with a combination of regret and sadness in her voice. "But you used to be friends." Hannah said nothing, so Martha tried again. "Could you maybe just try?"

"Mom." Hannah said softly as she looked up at her mother.

"Yes?"

"Maggie made her feelings clear, back at the end of July—about what I was going through, and how I was being selfish, getting all the attention at school, just because my grandfather died!"

Hannah was nearly shouting. She was trying so hard to not let her anger, sadness, emptiness and pain boil up from the wall that she hid them behind. But a single tear escaped and slid slowly down her right cheek.

Martha moved her arm around Hannah's shoulders and squeezed lightly. "I know that. Well, I didn't know all of that, but I knew some of it."

Hannah sniffled.

"In that case, if you don't want to talk to her, you don't have to." When Hannah looked up at her, she added,

"And if you decide you do want to talk to her, you should tell her what you feel."

Hannah started to argue, but realized that what her mother had said actually sounded like a good plan.

So instead, she nodded. "Ok. Thanks mom."

Hannah reached up to hug her. She felt like her mom still did not understand completely how she felt about Maggie, but maybe a little more than she had a few minutes ago.

Hannah still felt like her heart was behind a wall, being torn apart, like it had been ripped into tiny pieces and those pieces had been lost and might never be found... She hoped it would change at some point. If it didn't, she feared she just might stay an empty shell forever.

"Why don't you go on out to the car, honey. I'll be there in a minute," Martha suggested. Hannah glanced at her mom, gave her a small smile, picked up her guitar case and cat carrier, then she turned away from her and walked out the revolving doors. Outside, her nine year old brother Ryan and her eleven year old sister Zoe sat in the back seat of their mom's car, and Maggie stood in front of the car... waiting for Hannah.

Maggie had dark blonde hair a lot like Hannah, but she had put blue highlights in her hair. Unlike Hannah, she was dressed fashionably. She wore black leggings, a short denim skirt and jacket that were strategically ripped, a red and black striped shirt and leather ankle boots with white fluff in them.

Since June, Maggie had been popular. She had designed the clothes for the school play and somehow attracted the popular girls in school. Suddenly, they wanted to be Maggie's best friends. Since then, Maggie had ignored Hannah more and more. And then to add insult to injury, the most popular guy had asked Maggie out on a date and after that, Maggie had been far too popular to hang out with Hannah.

Hannah and Maggie had never before been part of the popular crowd, but Maggie had always wanted to be.

She'd wanted to be queen of all the dances. She wanted to date the most popular guys in school and she wanted to go to the mall with the girlfriends who only cared about being fashionable and praising the queen bee.

Hannah used to joke with her that even being the queen of England wouldn't be enough for Maggie... and Maggie hadn't exactly disagreed, but she also hadn't really liked Hannah putting it that way, either.

After Hannah lost her grandfather in July, she'd started to miss Maggie more than she already had been. So Hannah had confronted Maggie and asked her why she ignored her so much.

Maggie had told her, "Well I found better people who like me, understand me and clearly have better fashion sense, and I don't see how you're so lonely, anyway. Everyone has been paying attention to you!"

Hannah couldn't believe what she was hearing. They had been best friends since Hannah's family had moved to New York.

She hadn't been able to stop herself from replying. "You do know I just lost my grandfather... and you're jealous because people feel sorry for me, and are trying to comfort me. Or are you afraid that I'm going to get too popular and steal your friends or your boyfriend!"

"You could never steal anything from me because my friends—and my boyfriend for that matter—would never associate with anything from a trash can!" Maggie had snapped back.

Hannah's heart felt like Maggie had just stabbed her. Hannah had actually put a hand over her chest where it hurt so much—half expecting to feel a knife sticking out of her chest... or at least the blood left behind from such a wound. There had been nothing there, which somehow made it worse. At least an actual wound would have been something to heal. The pain in her heart felt like it might never go away.

That was the moment that Hannah had created a wall around her heart. If this was all she was going to feel from now on... this intense pain, it would have to be better not to feel anything at all.

Maggie had stepped closer to Hannah and whispered in her ear. "You will never mean anything to my friends... or me, for that matter."

Maggie had smiled as if she had won a battle. Like she

had beaten Hannah into the ground and only Maggie stood victorious. Then she'd turned and walked back to her friends. But before she'd gone more than two steps, the words were tumbling out of Hannah's mouth. "How could you be such a monster!"

Maggie had turned to face Hannah. Her smile might have faltered just for a second—or it might have just been wishful thinking on Hannah's part—before Maggie shot back. "I guess when you have an annoying, pathetic, and lame friend for three years, you learn from your mistakes."

Then she'd turned away, flounced over to where her friends stood, waiting for her—and they'd all walked away, laughing.

Hannah's mom had tried to get them to reconcile. She'd tried to get Hannah to talk about it, but finally she stopped—or so Hannah thought.

Hannah knew there was no point. Maggie had made herself very clear. She had new friends now and was clearly not interested in having Hannah as a friend anymore.

So, Hannah had given up.

She really didn't see the point in trying to make someone be her friend, anyway. She was not someone who wanted fake friends. You were either a friend or you weren't. And Maggie wasn't—and never would be.

So, when her mom had said she might want to say goodbye to Maggie before they left, Hannah had felt zero interest. But since Mom had insisted, she would say goodbye.

She walked right over to Maggie, and looked her in the eye. "Good riddance."

A PAIN FROM THE PAST

Hannah walked away from the apartment building, moving closer to the car, but Maggie shifted her weight to make it obvious that she wasn't going to let Hannah pass her.

Hannah stopped walking. They were leaving today. Better to just get it over with. She sighed, rolled her eyes and set down her guitar case.

"What do you want, Maggie?" she asked, her voice as dry and emotionless as she could make it.

She tried to avoid looking at Maggie's face, but their eyes met before she could speak.

"I want my apology." Maggie said sharply.

Hannah's breath whooshed out as she stared at Maggie. Part of her wasn't completely surprised, but part of her was shocked that Maggie would pick this moment in time to be a selfish, entitled, little princess.

"Well you're not getting one because you don't deserve one." Hannah snapped as she crossed her arms and took a deep breath, physically and mentally preparing herself for battle.

"You think that it's okay to try to steal my friends and my boyfriend?" Maggie spat out.

Hannah nearly laughed. Was Maggie kidding... or was she actually serious?

"I did not try to steal your friends or your boyfriend, I never even liked your so-called friend—or your boyfriend—and I don't like any of the boys at our school. Even when you tried to fix me up with some of them, they were never my type. Oh, and by the way, you are the one who ignored me for an entire month before any of this happened. And I don't think I need to remind you again that I just lost my grandfather, who I was extremely close to, by the way. You haven't been much of a friend, much less a best friend, since June. I've been all alone, dealing with stupid school, and all that other stuff, plus Mom and Dad's divorce, for months!"

Hannah was nearly shouting by the end. Of all the times she had tried communicating with Maggie, she could not believe Maggie chose now to argue the point.

"Hit her, Hannah, hit her!" Ryan, Hannah's little brother, called out from behind Maggie. Clearly he had been watching and listening to them.

Hannah hid her smile at her brother's comment. It was the first time she'd felt like smiling in weeks.

Inside the car, Hannah's younger sister, Zoe, tried to get Ryan to stop watching and give Hannah some privacy, but since Ryan never listened to her, she didn't really expect any different behavior from him. She decided to ignore him, turning her face away from the window.

A moment later, Maggie took a step closer to Hannah. "This conversation is all I need to know that we will never be friends again." She started to turn away, but swung back around suddenly.

"And by the way, you never told me your type. And as for your grandfather, he probably brought his death on himself."

While Hannah sputtered, she kept going. "He always went on and on about that stupid haunted house. A ghost probably just scared him, made him swerve and hit the guardrail."

At least she was speaking softly now, leaning very close to Hannah, so that her brother and sister couldn't hear her cruel words.

Of course, then she smiled and turned, starting to walk away in that self-confident way she had taught herself to do. Hannah remembered when she'd been working it all out—teaching herself to do it. It was all a sham. At least Hannah knew that.

And since she'd had it with Maggie, she didn't see any reason not to give Ryan a little bit of what he'd wanted. At first, she tightened her fist, but the memory of that doorknob crumpling in her fist stopped her. Instead, she marched after Maggie, moved in front of her—and then kicked her in the shin.

Maggie yelled and dropped to the ground.

Ryan leaped out of his seat, his fists in the air, shouting, "Yes!" Zoe pulled him back from the window, shoving him toward his seat, where he continued to shout and pump his fists in the air.

Then she called out to her sister. "Hannah!" A second

later, she was opening her car door behind the passenger seat and rushing around the car to where Hannah stood.

"Are you ok?" Zoe asked when she reached her sister. She put her hand on Hannah's shoulder, completely ignoring the whimpering sounds Maggie was making as she curled up on the sidewalk in front of their apartment building.

Zoe may have been nothing more than Hannah's nerdy little sister, but she always seemed to take the right side in a fight.

"I'm not hurt; well, not physically." Hannah said as she looked at Maggie on the concrete sidewalk, holding her right leg.

It was impossible to tell if her pain was genuine. Maggie had fake cried so many times, that she'd adopted the fake ones as her real tears.

It was also possible that Hannah just didn't have any sympathy for Maggie anymore.

"Why are you asking if she's hurt, I'm the one on the ground with a broken leg! She doesn't have a scratch on her!" Maggie said and then moaned again.

"Hannah doesn't lie, Maggie, or do you need a famous actor to tell you that so you'd actually believe it?" Zoe defended her sister.

Fortunately, she never seemed to mind being snidely blunt to people who hurt others.

"I can't feel my leg!" Maggie whined.

Zoe turned back to Hannah and rolled her eyes.

Hannah cringed. She'd tried to not hit her too hard, but she feared she might have actually broken Maggie's leg. Six months ago, she would have just assumed Maggie was being a big baby, but since their grandfather's funeral... her strength had been doing strange things.

Once or twice she had been tempted to tell Zoe, with her being such a sci-fi book nerd. But Hannah hadn't actually gotten up the nerve to tell her yet—to tell anyone yet. Part of it was fear of scaring her baby sister and forever destroying any type of good relationship they may have. Part of it was just fear that she might actually just scar her sister for life—what with everything that had happened to Zoe in her relatively short life so far.

"Everything okay, you guys?" Martha asked as she came out of the apartment building doors and approached the car.

"Maggie thinks her leg is broken." Zoe answered, not sounding sympathetic at all. She sounded annoyed—at

Maggie, which gave Hannah a strange, warm feeling she didn't try to explain or understand. She just enjoyed it. Perhaps Zoe was stronger than Hannah had given her credit for.

"Oh. " Martha said. "Well we'd better get going."

Martha watched Maggie as she walked to the back of the car, putting the two boxes she'd been carrying into the back of it. She seemed to be making a scene, but there was nothing truly worrying about her behavior. She'd certainly seen enough of Maggie's little spells to know that the girl had a wide drama streak. When Maggie said nothing to her, she felt sure that this was one of them. She shrugged her shoulders and walked around the car to get in the driver's seat.

Zoe opened her car door to get in, but waited for Hannah, who waved her hand at Ryan, who had scooted over behind her seat, to motion for him to scoot over. He didn't want to, but he rolled his eyes and followed his older sister's command. He scooted back over to sit behind the driver's seat.

Before Hannah could turn toward the car, Maggie pushed herself to her feet and stood... maybe a little unsteady, but certainly not with a broken leg.

Hannah turned away, moving to get into the car but Maggie grabbed her arm.

"You're a witch Hannah, a witch, I guess it runs in the family, since your grandfather was one, too." Maggie spoke just loud enough for her to hear, though Zoe was watching their exchange intently.

Hannah's fist tightened instinctively again, but she resisted the urge to punch Maggie. She had meant to kick the girl who had once masqueraded as her best friend, but she didn't really want to hurt her... not really. She took a deep breath before moving closer to Maggie.

"At least I'm not a ditzy brat, Maggie." She spoke quietly.

Maggie looked dumbstruck for about a second, then she huffed. She was trying to look annoyed and self-assured, snotty as usual, but there was something else in her eyes. Hannah could see that Maggie had no idea what "ditsy" meant.

It was a good feeling.

"Goodbye, Maggie." Hannah said in a normal, even tone. Then she turned to the car. Pumpkin leaped in ahead of her and Hannah followed, closing the door behind her.

Before they drove away Hannah leaned out the open window. Pumpkin pushed up beside her, watching Maggie.

"Witch's dog." Maggie snarled.

Pumpkin looked up at Hannah, she almost believed the look on her dog's face was her asking Hannah to open the car and let her attack Maggie. Hannah smiled at the thought, but didn't give in to it. A second later, she rolled up her window. "Not now, Pumpkin. She's not worth it."

It was then that she realized she actually felt better, standing up to Maggie. Finally, she had faced one of the things in her life that had broken her soul. And she hadn't backed down.

BROOKLYN

LEAVING MANHATTAN

Hannah looked out the window as they headed down the street, weaving their way through the area she had finally started to think of as home.

When they had moved to New York, Hannah had been convinced she could never feel at home there. But in the time they had been there, she had finally started to feel like it was indeed home.

Now they were driving away, leaving Manhattan behind, heading toward Brooklyn.

Mom had said the plan was to spend a night in

Brooklyn with Hannah's uncle. One last night in New York before they left the city and the state behind—forever.

Forever... because the next morning, she, Zoe, Ryan and their mom, would head to a small town in Connecticut—a place called Shadowhill.

It was the town where Hannah's grandfather had grown up. Apparently, quite a few generations had lived there, going almost all the way back to the start of the country. The house he had lived in hadn't actually been there since the Colonial days, but he had assured her at least part of it had been built back then.

Evidently, over the years, they had added on to that house. Hannah had never seen any pictures, but when she thought about it, she always pictured several houses rammed up against each other in a haphazard, ramshackle fashion.

One of her grandfather's favorite stories was about the first generation to live there just after the sinking of the Titanic. It was interesting to hear about, but it always made Hannah stop and think about that time and how different it was from now.

If Hannah had been on the Titanic, what class would she have been staying? Would she have survived? Or would she have been one of the misfortunate ones lost at sea?

It was more than a little creepy knowing that some of your ancestors had drowned on a ship and were still lying at the bottom of the ocean. She was grateful that some had survived—though Grandpa had never really talked about who did—and who did not.

He had spoken only of those who lived in the house just after the sinking occurred.

"You okay?" Zoe asked, looking over at Hannah, pulling her out of her thoughts.

Zoe had been showing her concern for Hannah more and more ever since Maggie had chucked her for the "in crowd." Though Zoe had never really had friends outside her family, she obviously felt sympathy for her sister.

Especially since Zoe had expressed a want for more friends of her own in the past—and she'd never really had any.

This past New Years Eve, Hannah and Maggie had taken Zoe out to a party at one of the fancy apartments where one of the most popular guys from school lived.

Martha had encouraged Zoe to go, so she could make some friends. Zoe had gone and mostly walked around by herself. She had talked with a few people, but it hadn't really been much of a surprise to Hannah that she'd not found anyone who shared her likes or dislikes, given the crowd there. Even Hannah hadn't had a great time. She'd mostly been stuck trying to get away from an arranged date that Maggie had set her up with.

Maggie had told her mother that she was going to a party with Hannah and Zoe, since her mother wouldn't let her go any other way, but Maggie had pretty much ignored Zoe and Hannah from the moment they'd walked in the door—so she could spend the entire evening snogging with one of the boys at the party.

"I'm fine." Hannah said through gritted teeth.

She never meant to be harsh with her family, but memories of Maggie had a way of getting on Hannah's last nerve. Something about the memory of their grandfather's story... thinking of the classes on that ship, must have made her remember that night when Zoe had interrupted her thoughts.

Hannah had to admit she did feel a little better after standing up to Maggie, but there were just too many memories with her ex so-called best friend. And driving through Manhattan, where so many of the memories had taken place, her nerves still on edge, and with so much weighing down on her, she couldn't help but remember.

Before she could go back down memory lane though,

Ryan shouted.

"Mom, Hannah's being mean!"

She looked over at her brother. What had she done to him? He didn't answer, just stuck his tongue out at her.

"No, she's not. Leave her alone." Zoe said, calmly defending her sister.

Martha only sighed as she navigated through the New York traffic—trying to stay as calm as possible. She had been hoping the sibling rivalry would be down to a minimum, but to her disappointment, her son had other ideas. And she knew it would get worse seeing his cousins who were around the same age as he. But Martha wasn't going to put the visit off.

Her sister-in-law was planning special foods in honor of their arrival and she hadn't seen her brother since the funeral. They were moving a hundred and forty miles away from their family here. Who knew when they'd be back again for a visit.

Hannah took deep breaths all the way to Brooklyn, trying to calm down. She didn't want to be tense around her Uncle Darryl, his wife, and his kids. She wanted to do everything she could to enjoy the visit.

After about a forty-minute drive due to the traffic, they arrived in Brooklyn. The gravel driveway crunched under their tires. Hannah grabbed hold of her sleeping bag and her duffle bag, pulling them with her as she got out of the car. She kept a tight hold on Pumpkin's leash. Zoe got her backpack and sleeping bag, then got out of the back of the car, as Ryan did the same.

Martha took several deep breaths before getting out of the car and walking around to the back where she retrieved her own sleeping bag and her small overnight bag. They all closed their respective doors at about the same time. They looked around at each other at the sound of all the doors closing at once. After a second, they all laughed.

Martha pressed the lock button on her key fob and the car beeped once. She'd gotten used to locking whatever car she was driving. It was mainly a habit, the need to always lock her car, since she'd lived in New Orleans, Nashville and New York at different points in her life.

They all stood near the car, looking at the house. The brown exterior, the arched opening to the front porch, the big, beautiful windows, the one small clouded window, which Hannah remembered was the bathroom window. The rest of the windows were mostly covered by curtains, even the upstairs windows. The house almost looked like a stretched out gingerbread house.

The roof in front came to a point, one smaller triangle above the arched entrance to the porch, and another off to the side, slightly taller than the other.

At the window, to the right of the front door, a small face appeared, then the person rushed away from the window. In just a few seconds the front door opened and a little girl came running out the door.

The little girl had brown hair with dark blonde highlights, pale skin and green eyes. She wore a pink skirt, white tennis shoes, a white shirt with hot pink frilly short sleeves, with a picture of a unicorn from a cartoon television show on her shirt.

"Zoe!" The little girl came running down the steps of the porch and over to Zoe. She wrapped her arms around Zoe's waist. Zoe was quite a bit taller than her young cousin.

"Hey Pammy." Zoe hugged her. Pammy was the youngest daughter of their uncle. Though Zoe had never really had friends outside the family, Pammy had always seen her as a buddy.

"Pammy, jacket!" A woman walked out the front door, holding a pink jacket.

This was Martha's sister-in-law, Naomi. She was the opposite of most women who married men with sisters. Naomi actually liked Martha. Before Martha had married and moved all over the country, they were quite close. Whenever Uncle Darryl, Martha's brother, would go to work, Martha would come over to their house and help Aunt Naomi with the kids.

"I don't need it." Pammy argued, letting go of Zoe.

Zoe said nothing, just stood there with her hand on Pammy's shoulder.

Pammy sighed heavily. Clearly, she didn't want her mom hovering while she hung out with her cool cousin.

"Hello, Martha." Aunt Naomi said, walking over to Martha and hugging her.

The two women held each other close for a long hug. They hadn't seen each other since Christmas Eve. Naomi had tried to make it to the funeral, but she'd had to work.

"Hi, Naomi." Martha said as Naomi walked over and draped the pink jacket over Pammy's shoulders.

Zoe gave her cousin a look when she started to shrug back out of the jacket. Pammy sighed, but didn't argue with her cool cousin.

A moment later, Uncle Darryl walked out of the house and two boys scrambled out the door behind him and ran over to Ryan. These two young boys were Uncle Darryl and Aunt Naomi's sons, Cole and Henry. Uncle Darryl rolled his eyes at his sons' haste to get over to their cousin and cause trouble for them all to deal with.

Cole had black hair, and he wore a red shirt with dark blue sleeves and blue jeans. Henry had dark brown hair and was wearing a dark green shirt, with yellow sleeves and dark blue jeans.

Uncle Darryl looked over at his younger sister and smiled, as he walked over to Martha and hugged her.

"Hey Darryl." Martha said, leaning into the hug her brother wrapped her in.

"Hey sis." Uncle Darryl smiled as he hugged his sister.

Right then, Uncle Darryl's oldest daughter, Tilly, walked out onto the porch. She had brown hair, and she wore a green short-sleeve shirt, blue jeans, and black tennis shoes with white toes. And unlike Hannah, her eyes were glued to her phone as she walked out of the house.

"Hi." Tilly said. Her voice was emotionless and

distracted. She wasn't paying attention to anyone, unless, of course, she was paying attention to someone on her phone.

"Hey Tilly!" Hannah waved, despite Tilly not paying attention.

Hannah looked around at all of her cousins. The oldest was Tilly at seventeen. Next was Cole and Henry at ten years old. Pammy was the youngest, who had just turned six years old.

She was going to miss them all so much when they moved away.

"You wanna go up to our room?" Henry asked Ryan. "Sure." Ryan said with excitement in his voice. He caught up to them and followed them into the house.

"Boys, don't wear out Ryan!" Aunt Naomi hollered after her sons. "And don't be getting into any trouble."

Zoe laughed at her aunt's words. She knew they had a tendency to get into trouble. Her trying to stop it before it started would probably be a waste of breath.

Still, Zoe supposed it was worth a try.

"Come on in." Uncle Darryl walked toward the house with Martha at his side as Aunt Naomi moved to Martha's other side. Pammy raised her arms up to Zoe, who smiled and picked her up.

"You've gotten heavier." Zoe said and let out a groan.

She shifted her cousin's weight to her other leg and tightened her hold on Pammy, who hugged tightly to Zoe and smiled. Zoe smiled back at her cousin and then followed the parents up to the house.

Hannah sighed, then followed them inside. She walked into the living room and closed the front door behind her. The living room was dark, the curtains were closed, none of the lamps were on. Light only came from the kitchen and from down the hall.

From the noise above their heads, Hannah assumed that her brother and cousins were causing some sort of chaos in their room. She shook her head and followed everyone through the main room.

Across from the front door were floor to ceiling glass windows. In the middle of the windows was a glass door leading to the back yard, but with the curtains drawn, Hannah could not see them.

Though the living room floor was carpeted, a blanket laid on the floor. Zoe and Pammy had already settled on the blanket and were playing with Pammy's doll house. Tilly was still on her phone, sprawled in a chair next to the front door, mindlessly staring at her phone and typing out messages.

"Tilly, go get the boys and tell them that lunch is almost ready." Aunt Naomi told her daughter. Tilly sighed the way Hannah had heard Maggie sigh so many times, making it clear that Tilly was annoyed. She got out of her chair with a heavy sigh, turned to the left and headed up the stairs.

"Would it be okay for me to let Pumpkin off her leash?" Hannah asked.

"Oh yeah, just keep her away from the boys room, we don't want them feeding her clay." Aunt Naomi said with a wave of her hand.

"Okay." Hannah knelt down and unhooked Pumpkin's leash from her collar.

Pammy crawled over to Pumpkin and rubbed the dog's face. Pammy seemed happy, but then again, what did she have to worry about, being only six.

"I hope you like tacos." Aunt Naomi turned toward the kitchen. "We just bought them yesterday." She went on as she continued on to the kitchen.

"Hey Martha, can I talk to you?" Uncle Darryl asked, holding Martha's right elbow and nodding his head to his left, toward their dining room.

Martha nodded, and moved with her brother. They both walked the rest of the way across the room and into the dining room.

Zoe watched them suspiciously. Hannah looked at Zoe, wondering what was going on in her head. But before she could figure it out, her train of thought was interrupted by Ryan, Cole and Henry running into the room. All three boys were making as much noise as they could, with Tilly walking quietly behind them, rolling her eyes and sighing.

Hannah had sighed that way about her brother more than once, but she didn't dare comment on her brother and younger cousins' loudness, because Ryan would be louder just to spite Hannah, therefore encouraging Henry and Cole to be louder and make faces at Hannah. Ryan, being the irrepressible boy that he is, seemed to enjoy doing things to get on Hannah and Zoe's nerves.

AMONG FAMILY

Zoe looked down at Pammy, who was happily playing with Pumpkin. Zoe glanced up at the dining room, and tried to listen to her mother's and uncle's hushed conversation. But when she couldn't hear them, she decided to try to snoop.

Zoe stood up as nonchalantly as she could and walked out of the living room, down the short hall, turned left and walked into the kitchen, over to where her Aunt Naomi stood. She looked past Aunt Naomi and saw her mother and uncle talking.

After just a few seconds, Uncle Darryl saw her. He took her mother's arm and they both went into another room—one out of Zoe's sight. Zoe sighed. Her mother had been different all this last year. Normally, she would assume that it was because of the divorce and losing her father, but she'd been different even before that.

Zoe suspected that her father had cheated on her mother and perhaps she knew but didn't tell anyone. The thought of her father cheating on her mother made her sick, but she wasn't surprised. For some reason, her father had always seemed distant with her for some reason, too.

It always seemed like Hannah and Ryan got extra hugs, but when she'd try to get closer to her father, he was always "busy with something else." Zoe had approached Hannah with the idea, but until recently Hannah hadn't believed her.

"When will the food be done?" Zoe asked, turning her attention to her Aunt Naomi, giving a sensible reason for being in the kitchen, other than to spy on her mom and uncle, anyway.

"Soon. A few minutes." Aunt Naomi answered, focusing on the stovetop.

"Okay." Zoe turned to leave the kitchen.

"I've tried." Aunt Naomi said, which caused Zoe to stop and turn around to look at Aunt Naomi, attempting to not look intrigued or too curious.

"What?" Zoe asked. She tried to sound like she wasn't eavesdropping and truly interested in dinner. But her curiosity always won out.

"I've tried to eavesdrop." Aunt Naomi said, turning to face Zoe, leaving dinner in the back of both of their minds. "You'd have to be psychic to hear their conversations."

Her face was so serious. Aunt Naomi knew that her husband and sister-in-law were talking about something possibly life altering, not what you would expect from a brother and sister who just saw each other a few months ago.

"Yeah, you should have heard some of the conversations my mom and dad had." Zoe told her aunt, nodding her head, trying to release the tension rising in her stomach. "Not that I actually heard what they were talking about, but they talked privately a lot. And they were always asking us to leave the room." Zoe said, looking down.

The idea of something serious going on with her family

made her stomach do cartwheels.

"Well unfortunately, psychics don't exist in this world." Aunt Naomi said quietly.

Zoe could tell that her aunt was trying to bring up her spirits. "Yeah." Zoe laughed, looking off to the side, then turned and walked out into the hall. "In this world." She said quietly, then walked back into the living room.

She remembered feelings of yearning for a life of adventure, passing the hours by reading science fiction and fantasy books filled with adventure. She always wanted a life of adventure, but the idea of her mother and uncle talking over things like divorce and love affairs that her father may have gone through to hurt her mother, wounded Zoe. She wondered if she could handle sword battles, quests and saving lives, especially since she had longed for that type of escape when her mother had told her that they were getting divorced.

"Tilly, come set the table!" Aunt Naomi hollered from the kitchen. Tilly rolled her eyes and sighed as she turned her phone off. Uncrossing her legs, she got up and walked past Zoe and Pammy playing on the floor with Pumpkin, and went into the kitchen.

Henry, Cole and Ryan ran down the stairs and past Zoe and Pammy. Pumpkin lifted her head as their footsteps pounded past her, her tail wagging.

Zoe sighed, knowing that whatever the three menaces were plotting, they were likely to drive her aunt into insanity.

Hannah sighed wearily. Zoe looked over at her sister, as Hannah got up and walked over to the glass door across from where Zoe and Pammy were petting Pumpkin.

Hannah opened the glass door and went outside, leaving Zoe with her curiosity. Even though they were not close in their teen and tween hood, Zoe and Hannah had been close as children. They had always banded together and played with legos and stuffed animals.

But there was also something about the time Hannah had saved Zoe from drowning in Lake Rikersfield. It had brought them even closer.

Zoe looked down to the carpet at the memory of that experience—of being pulled under the water by something that had taken hold of her ankle…

She had been drifting out on the lake, lying on a float. Her family was splashing nearby, teaching Ryan to swim. The sun was right above her, warming her skin as she floated lazily across the water, enjoying the chance to just zone out and enjoy the time all to herself.

And before she knew what was happening, before she could even make a sound, something had taken hold of her ankle and yanked her off the float and down into the water.

Deeper into the depths she had gone—being pulled so fast, it had taken her too long to realize what was happening. She had barely started struggling when the intense cold had started to frighten her. How deep was she by then? How would she get to the surface before running out of air?

The burning of the water in her lungs...

And then the loneliness... watching the light fade as she was pulled deeper. That was the worst of all...

Had anyone even noticed she was gone? Would they notice before it was too late? How would she get away from whatever it was that was pulling her downward?

That's when she looked down, to see what had hold of her, before she completely lost the light. And she would never forget what she saw down below her, deeper in the water… The bright, glowing green eyes that would sear themselves forever into her memories—and her nightmares.

Zoe looked up at the feeling of a small hand on her shoulder.

Pammy.

She had a worried look on her face. "Zoe, are you okay?" Pammy asked, her face looking more and more worried. Zoe noticed Pumpkin's paw on her knee, but although she was looking at Pammy, Zoe could swear the dog looked worried too.

"I'm fine!" Zoe said as enthusiastically as she could, with a wide smile on her face.

Worried about her young cousin, she ruthlessly pushed her memories as far away as she could. There was no reason that her six-year old cousin should have to be worried about her.

After a few more seconds, Pammy moved her hand,

but still looked skeptical. Finally, she went back to paying attention to Pumpkin again.

Even though they were four years apart in age, Zoe always got along better with Pammy than she did with her peers.

It was handy since occasionally her aunt and uncle would drop the two boys off with their grandmother and they'd usually drop Pammy off to hang out with Zoe. Sometimes they even had sleepovers.

Hannah was rarely with Zoe when she babysat, because she was usually with Maggie at the latest popular party. Aunt Naomi would always tell Zoe that she was very mature for her age and since Zoe loved spending time with Pammy, she would pay her to babysit.

Their mom had usually been busy with her job, or with the few chances she got to do something for herself—like when she'd make an appointment for a spa day.

Whenever Zoe would hang out with Pammy. Her dad, John, would take Ryan out for father and son time.

A couple of times when Zoe hadn't been babysitting, Hannah had dragged her to a party, so that she could meet and spend time with her peers—mostly to have a chance at trying to find friends of her own.

Zoe never had.

No one at those parties understood her quirky type of personality, or the fact that Zoe would rather have her nose stuck in a book than be at those parties in the first place. And there were absolutely no guys who were interested in Zoe. Hannah had introduced Zoe to guys at every party and they'd endured her for a few minutes and then made a smooth exit. It seemed like all the guys crowded around girls like Hannah... and Maggie.

Hannah was skinny, with medium blonde hair and, even though she wasn't one of the popular kids, she was pretty enough to be on the "respected by the popular kids" level.

Zoe, on the other hand, wasn't fat, but she wasn't skinny, either. Zoe had noticeable hips and unlike many girls her age, she was more developed in her chest... only because she had hit puberty when she was ten.

Zoe's mother always told her that she was beautiful and Zoe believed her, but it always seemed like guys wanted Hannah instead of Zoe. Martha told her that it didn't help Zoe with the popular kids when they all wore ridiculous amounts of makeup and all Zoe would wear was lip gloss and sometimes she didn't even bother with that, because it was just gonna get rubbed off when she ate.

Zoe suspected that was another reason guys preferred Hannah. She—especially when spending time with Maggie—would wear makeup and try to fit in with the popular kids.

Zoe refused to. She wanted to be her own person.

"Henry, don't put taco shells in your brother's hair!" Aunt Naomi yelled from the kitchen.

Zoe looked toward the kitchen with a gasp. Ryan got into trouble often enough, but thankfully, he'd never tried to put tacos in her or her sister's hair.

Pammy didn't even look up. She just went on, gently stroking Pumpkin's back.

A second later we heard, "Cole, don't put apple juice in there!" Aunt Naomi yelled again. A loud clatter came from the direction of the kitchen just after her words.

Pammy just sat there, looking as if this was a normal, everyday occurrence in their house.

"Henry, get that sauce out of your hair!" Aunt Naomi yelled. Zoe looked back to her cousin and smiled at the craziness.

"But now I have taco hair." Henry answered calmly.

"No, now you just need meat." Cole told him.

"Cole, get that meat out of your pocket!" Aunt Naomi insisted, after which Cole said something Zoe couldn't hear.

"What do you mean that's not meat?" Aunt Naomi asked, sounding only slightly calmer, but confused at the same time.

A few minutes of silence passed, and then the sound of giggling came from the kitchen.

"That is not funny, get that meat out of your pocket!" Aunt Naomi hollered as Henry and Cole ran out of the kitchen from the connecting side to the dining room.

Aunt Naomi walked out a few seconds behind them, but Cole and Henry ran away from her and past Zoe and Pammy, heading toward the stairs.

"Henry, you come back with those sweets right now!" Aunt Naomi hollered after them.

Henry and Cole bumped into Ryan, who had just

started down the stairs from the boy's room.

"She didn't fall for it." Henry told them, holding the meat from Cole's pocket in his hand.

"Only because you wouldn't stop giggling." Cole said, standing behind Henry, glaring at his brother, with his arms crossed.

"Only because I was imagining the look on her face." Henry insisted.

"Boys." Aunt Naomi called out to them.

"Come on." Henry said.

"Let's go." Cole said, almost at the same time as Henry spoke.

Then Henry, Ryan and Cole ran back upstairs to Henry and Cole's room.

"Darryl!" Aunt Naomi hollered, and less than five seconds later Uncle Darryl walked up behind Aunt Naomi and stood at her side.

"Yes, dear?" Uncle Darryl asked, breathing a little heavily, from rushing over to her.

"You need to deal with your sons." Aunt Naomi told him, emphasizing on "you" and "deal" and last but not least "your sons."

And then she walked back into the kitchen after poking Uncle Darryl in the chest with her index finger. Uncle Darryl sighed and then mumbled something and headed upstairs toward Cole and Henry's room.

Tilly walked back into the living room, sat down on the couch and pulled out her phone.

"And we thought we had problems." Zoe said.

"Oh you do, we've never had to live through a divorce." Tilly said as Hannah opened the back door, came inside and closed the door behind her.

"Gratefully." Hannah said as she passed Tilly and sat next to her on the couch.

"The only divorce we'd want is from Cole and Henry." Pammy said.

"Only some of the time." Tilly said. In a hushed tone to Hannah, she whispered, "Most of the time."

"I'd second that." Zoe whispered, holding her hand up then dropping it to her lap.

Hannah nodded, smiling and agreeing with her sister. Hannah felt a bit odd, hanging out with Zoe, since they usually only spent about ten minutes a day around each other.

And Zoe was usually found with a book in her hands, her eyes carefully soaking up every word. It was not unusual to see Zoe with a different book every day, sometimes even, a new book within a few hours... depending on the book.

She could finish a normal book in hours, though she preferred bigger books—mammoth things that weighed as much or more than some of their school books. Those she usually finished within a day or two.

After a few minutes, Aunt Naomi called everyone into the dining room to eat.

Pammy shifted her weight and Pumpkin crawled off of her lap as Zoe stood up and helped her cousin up. Zoe and Pammy led the way to the dining room, Hannah and Tilly right behind them, arms interlocked.

Tilly's walk was bold, sure of herself. Hannah's walk was weak, and limp. It looked as if Tilly was holding Hannah up. Zoe glanced behind her and saw Hannah.

She worried about her sister.

Aunt Naomi was putting several bowls on the dining table... one with green beans, one with Mexican rice, another with refried beans and one with taco meat. The rest of the fixings for tacos were already on the table... taco shells, lettuce, shredded cheese, sour cream, and three bottles of different types of hot sauce.

Zoe put her hands on the back of the chair where she intended to sit and Pammy climbed onto the chair next to it. All of the boys ran into the dining room with Uncle Darryl right behind them. Cole just stood for a few seconds, then went and sat down in the chair two down from Pammy. Henry then went and sat down next to Cole and Ryan sat down next to Cole.

Martha came out of the kitchen just as Hannah and Tilly walked into the dining room. Hannah sat down in the chair on the other side of Zoe and Tilly sat next to Hannah.

"We need more chairs." Martha announced, then she and Uncle Darryl went back into the room where they had been talking ten minutes ago.

A minute later, they each came back with two more wooden chairs.

"Tilly, Hannah, Zoe, could you scoot closer to

Pammy?" Martha asked the girls.

Zoe, Hannah and Tilly moved their chairs closer to Pammy. Martha set down the two chairs next to Tilly and on the other side of the two chairs were another empty chair. Martha sat down next to Ryan, then Uncle Darryl came and sat down next to Tilly. Aunt Naomi finished things up in the kitchen and put something in the fridge, then walked into the dining room and sat in between Martha and Uncle Darryl.

"So." Uncle Darryl reached for two taco shells. "How is school so far?"

"Good, so far." Tilly added meat to her taco shell. Cole, Henry and Ryan didn't reply, since they were busy putting hot sauce on their taco shells, then meat, then more taco sauce.

Pammy rolled her eyes at her brother's choices.

"What exactly is your plan for school?" Uncle Darryl directed his question at Hannah, Zoe and Martha, Hannah opened her mouth to speak, but stopped when her mom replied.

"I actually pulled them out of school so we could get settled, so I'm homeschooling them until after Christmas." Martha answered as she put together a taco.

Uncle Darryl nodded. He looked for a minute like he wanted to say something, but either he changed his mind or he decided to let it go because his wife spoke up then.

"Won't that be hard on them, being in a new school after the new year has started?" Aunt Naomi asked.

"I had that thought." This, she directed toward Naomi specifically. Then she added, That's why I thought it would be better to start after they come back from Christmas break. At least then they'll all be starting a new semester."

Aunt Naomi, motioning toward Uncle Darryl, added. "I guess I just don't understand why all of this had to happen so quickly. Why you can't let them finish the school year here and then move."

Martha shrugged a little as she answered. "It's really the best we could do in this situation." Her tone was sad now, her voice quiet.

"Well then, if you're homeschooling them now, why wouldn't it be better to..."

Martha interrupted. "I'm not worried about it and neither is Hannah, Zoe or Ryan."

"That you know of." Hannah whispered.

Zoe looked toward Hannah, with her head tilted

down. No one else seemed to hear Hannah's comment.

"Why can't we live here?" Ryan asked.

"Because we moved out of our apartment and the new people have probably already signed their lease." Martha said.

"But why can't we live here, with Uncle Darryl and Aunt Naomi?" Ryan asked. "I don't have any brothers and Cole and Henry are fun." Ryan whined.

"We can't impose on them and we need to get our own place." Martha said. Ryan looked down at his food, dejectedly.

"There is a place next door you could look at." Aunt Naomi said.

Ryan's head whipped up, his eyes full of hope.

"And a place down the street, too." Aunt Naomi added.

"Yes, that's true." Uncle Darryl added, nodding his head, his voice clearly full of excitement at the thought of his sister and her family living closer to them.

Hannah and Zoe knew the true reason why their mom didn't want to stay in New York. She wanted to make a different life, without her now ex-husband. A life where she didn't depend on someone else for her life and possibly for her happiness.

Hannah and Zoe didn't tell anyone else this—just like they hadn't mentioned it to their mom.

But they still knew the truth.

COMFORTING HONESTY

After lunch Martha, Uncle Darryl and Aunt Naomi stayed in the kitchen doing dishes and talking quietly.

Hannah and Tilly went off to the room Tilly and Pammy shared. Ryan ran off with the other boys to play in their room.

Zoe and Pammy slowly wandered from the dining room to the living room. "Do you want to go outside and play?" Pammy asked.

"Sure, why not." Zoe answered. She followed Pammy outside to the trampoline.

They bounced on it for a long time before the heavy meal they'd eaten started to feel uncomfortable from all the bouncing.

Pammy flopped down and stretched out on the trampoline, her arms and legs spread out. She sighed dramatically, in the way only a young child can do. Zoe had heard the same thing from Ryan many times. It was the sigh that said a thousand other things... mostly meaning he wanted attention for some reason.

Zoe took one last jump, tucking her legs under herself and landed next to her cousin. They both still shook a little from the echoes of their bouncing as the trampoline settled.

"Zoe." Pammy rolled over onto her stomach and faced her cousin, holding her arms straight in front of her chest.

"Does every marriage end in divorce?" Her face was a mask of sadness and worry, her voice the same.

"No, of course not." Zoe replied, realizing that Pammy must eavesdrop on her parents the way Zoe did with her own parents.

"Why do you ask?" Zoe asked, concerned for her

young cousin.

"Do you think my parents will get a divorce?" Pammy asked, tears behind her eyes, her voice quivering a little as she spoke.

"Oh honey, of course not." Zoe reassured her, wrapping her hand around her cousin's small hands.

"Then why did your parents get divorced?" Pammy asked, still sounding tearful.

Zoe considered her words carefully. It was the first time she had really thought about it from someone else's perspective. She had wondered many times over the last few months why her parents divorced and she always came up with the same answer.

"I always kinda guessed that they didn't have the same feelings for each other as they did when they met, so they didn't want to be tied to each other any more." Zoe carefully explained to her six year old cousin.

Pammy watched her cousin as Zoe explained and then nodded her head solemnly.

"I have learned that divorce is a ridiculously complicated situation. I don't know that a person can really understand it all until they've been through it." Zoe added.

"I'm not sure I want to be in that type of situation."

"Me neither." Zoe said. Then added, with a half smile and a wistfulness in her voice. "I guess all we can do is pray that we never have to be in that kind of situation ourselves."

"So you really don't think that my parents will get divorced?" Pammy asked.

"I really don't. Your parents will love each other forever." Zoe answered her, smiling again at her young cousin.

She didn't say anything about death because she didn't want to frighten her young cousin. The conversation had already been so intense and kind of over Pammy's head, who was only six. Death was better left for another time.

"Come on, we've rested, let's jump some more." Zoe suggested, working to fill her voice with excitement.

"Okay." Pammy's voice told Zoe she wouldn't forget the conversation they'd just had, but maybe she felt a little better about it.

Zoe hoped so anyway.

They both jumped up and started bouncing again. Of course, not even ten minutes later, Zoe felt raindrops hitting her as they bounced.

"Pammy." Zoe said, bouncing a little less already.

"Yeah?" Pammy replied, clearly not noticing the raindrops.

"I think we need to go in."

"Why?" Pammy asked, her expression changing from happy to confused.

"It's starting to rain." Zoe answered, just as the rain started to pick up.

Zoe and Pammy stopped bouncing and carefully crawled out of the trampoline net as it started to really pour. Zoe wrapped her arms around her young cousin and hunched over to keep her dry as possible as they ran back into the house.

When they came back inside, Tilly looked up from her phone. "What happened? You're all wet."

"It started raining." Zoe told her, slightly out of breath.

A crash of thunder sounded outside, dangerously close. Pammy shrieked and tightened her hold of Zoe's shirt. Tilly walked over and looked out through the glass sliding doors.

"It's pouring, how are you not soaked?" Tilly asked.

"It must have picked up just when we closed the door, because it was only enough to get us drenched, I guess." Zoe said, ignoring Tilly's derisive tone.

"Good thing we came in when we did." Pammy said, looking outside, still holding tight to Zoe.

"Are you cold?" Hannah asked.

"A little." Pammy replied, looking at her older cousin.

Zoe nodded. "Yeah, a little."

"Come on, sit." Tilly said, moving closer to Pammy and Zoe. She motioned for both of them to sit down on the couch.

Zoe walked over to the couch, with Pammy still holding tightly onto her shirt. She knew that her young cousin had never liked thunder or lightning, so she didn't complain about the tight grip.

She sat down and took off her flip flops so she could put her feet under her and off to the side. Pammy took off her tennis shoes and did the same, only she added a little bounce to getting on the couch.

"Here you go," Hannah grabbed a blanket and draped it over Zoe and then Pammy, who was snuggled close to her cousin.

"There, that ought to warm you up."

Every time there was a crash of thunder outside, Pammy gripped harder onto Zoe. After a bit, her grip would relax, and then a crash of thunder would hit again.

Hannah turned on a movie to distract her sweet, little cousin. Thankfully, the combination of the movie distracting her—and the storm slowly moving off—had Pammy soon nodding off.

Not long after the movie ended, Pammy woke up when there was a knock at the front door. Tilly had just come downstairs from her room. She walked past them to answer the door.

When she opened the door, Daphne Matthews, Martha and Darryl's mother stood there with Lorena Autumn, the woman who had been Martha's mother-in-law.

"Granny!" Tilly said with excitement filling her voice.

"Gram!" Hannah said at about the same time.

Both teenagers rushed over to hug their grandmothers. Zoe turned off the TV, excited to see both her grandmothers. She tossed the blanket off and stood up. Pammy was just a second behind her springing off the couch.

"Hello, Tilly." Lorena said.

Zoe and Pammy walked over to take their turn hugging their grandmas.

"Pammy, sweetheart." Daphne leaned in to hug her granddaughter tightly.

At the same time, Lorena hugged Zoe. It could have been her imagination, but she thought her gram might have held on a little extra tight. She wondered why, but didn't ask.

"Can I take your coats?" Tilly asked.

"Oh sure." Lorena said. Tilly took Lorena's black coat that was completely soaked in water and then Daphne's dark sand colored coat that was also soaked in water. She hung them on hooks close to the front door so they could drip water on the rubber mat below the hooks, instead of the wood floor.

Daphne let her brown, gray streaked hair dangle She wore a black skirt with red and orange flowers, a red comfy sweater, and dark sand colored sandals.

Lorena's short, curly blonde hair with strands of gray, stopped just above her shoulders. Lorena wore blue jeans, a white shirt with colorful flowers, and white tennis shoes.

"Granny, Grams, what are you doing here?" Hannah asked.

"We came to see you before you left for Shadowhill. After all, we won't get to see you anytime we want once you move so far away." Lorena said, holding Hannah's hands.

"Till my birthday." Zoe wrapped her arms around Pammy, who stood in front of Zoe. Pammy held Zoe's hands, smiling.

"Yes, of course, dear." Lorena said.

"And we're all coming." Pammy said.

"Yes, we are. I'm trying to convince your aunt to come, too." Lorena said.

"Aunt Myra not wanting to come?" Zoe asked, rocking back and forth with Pammy.

"It's not that. She's still wrestling with her kids and she doesn't want to disrupt the school year. She does have three boys, after all." Lorena said.

"Well I have two and I make time for company to visit and do just fine." Aunt Naomi walked into the living room, with Martha right behind her.

"Hi, Mom." Aunt Naomi hugged Daphne.

"Yes, yes, we're aware, you have a lot of children." Daphne said.

"I'm just saying, would you want an extra boy in the house?" Lorena asked.

"I don't need it, I have two in the house right now. Three if you count my husband, not to mention Ryan." Aunt Naomi said, pointing behind her.

"Hi mom." Martha said, hugging Daphne.

"Hello, honey. How are you?" Daphne asked, trying not to make the divorce obvious, but Hannah and Zoe knew what she meant.

Tilly must have as well because her head dropped, as Zoe and Hannah looked around nervously. Pammy just started rocking back and forth, blissfully unaware of the tension in the room. Zoe rocked a little with her bliss-filled cousin.

"Speaking of which... where are the three little

terrors?" Lorena asked, her hands on her hips.

"Bedroom." Aunt Naomi motioned toward the stairs.

Lorena exclaimed happily and headed upstairs to the boy's room.

"And where is that man I call my son and your brother and your husband?" Daphne asked, toward Martha, then Aunt Naomi, hugging Martha by her side.

"He was in the boy's room." Aunt Naomi said.

"Excuse me, Lorena." Uncle Darryl said as he came down the hall and into the living room. "Mother." He walked toward her, his arms spread wide.

"Son." She turned to hug him.

"Brother." Martha joked as her brother hugged their mother.

"How've you been?" Daphne asked after they kissed each other on the cheeks.

"Fine." Uncle Darryl said.

"You will still be able to go to Shadowhill, for Zoe's birthday, right?" Daphne asked.

"Yes mother, I will." Uncle Darryl said.

"Obviously, I'll be able to make it." Martha said, then she and Daphne laughed.

"We wouldn't miss it for the world." Aunt Naomi reached out, taking Tilly into a side hug. "Come sit down." She said, motioning for Daphne to sit.

Zoe and Pammy sat back down where they had been sitting. Tilly and Hannah sat on the chair that was next to the couch, on the other side of the doorway to the dining room. "I'll be in the kitchen if anyone needs me." Aunt Naomi said, her hands together.

"As will I." Martha said, following Aunt Naomi into the kitchen, Uncle Darryl retreated back into the boys room.

The girls visited with Daphne. Or, at least Hannah and Zoe visited with her. Pammy went back to watching the movie she had mostly missed and Tilly watched her phone.

Lorena eventually escaped from the boy's room and rejoined them in the living room. They talked about the plans for Zoe's birthday, the girls' school plans, the move and all of the new friends they were going to make in Shadowhill.

They were all very careful to steer clear of any commentary about the divorce — and eventually, dinner was ready. Zoe turned off the movie over Pammy's protests, and they went to get their dinner.

When the boys came down, they took control of the television, turning on a game that Zoe really had no interest in. Despite that, they all ate in the living room, except for Martha, Daphne, Lorena and Aunt Naomi, who ate in the dining room.

Uncle Darryl, Zoe and Pammy sat on the couch. Uncle Darryl sat closer to the front door. Zoe sat closer to the living room, and Pammy sat in between them.

All of the boys sat on the floor watching the game on the television or playing with toy cars on the floor.

Tilly sat in the dark, velvet red chair that sat on the other side of the doorway to the living room. Hannah sat on the left arm of the chair.

"Zoe, you still don't want to go to San Francisco for your birthday, right?" Martha hollered from the dining room.

Zoe looked over at her mom. Martha shrugged a little, letting Zoe know that it was up to her.

"Right." Zoe answered.

Even though the game didn't really interest her all that much, she found herself watching it... even while hearing some of the conversation going on around her. She distantly heard her mom talking about her birthday and what she was going to try to talk Zoe's dad into doing for her birthday.

Their dad now lived in San Francisco. He was a lawyer, so that had been in his favor during the divorce. Their divorce had moved seemingly quick and he'd moved to San Francisco just as soon as it was over.

BELOVED SECRETS

After dinner was finished and the game was over, Daphne and Lorena decided it was time to leave.

"Martha, can I talk to you for a moment?" Daphne asked

She and Martha went into the hall that led to the kitchen and talked, while everyone said goodbye to Lorena. While they were gone, there was a flurry of hugs and goodbyes, voices raised and lots of laughter as the boys rushed around in between everyone.

When Daphne returned, the same round of hugs and goodbyes started over.

After several minutes, Daphne spoke up. "Oh for goodness sake, we'll be back tomorrow to see you off."

"You're right. Yes. OK kids, let's let Gram and Granny get home." Naomi said with a little laugh.

They all moved with Lorena and Daphne as they made their way to the door. The boys were the first ones to rush away. Tilly slipped out at some point, too.

"Zoe, could you walk us out?" Daphne asked, even though Lorena was already halfway to the car.

"Sure." Zoe took her grandmother's arm and walked her outside.

When they got outside, Lorena was already in the driver's seat. Halfway down the walk, Daphne stopped. Zoe looked back to see that, though the front door was closed, her mother and Aunt Naomi still stood on the front stoop.

Zoe looked up at her Gran with a question in her eyes. Why had she stopped and why right here—between the house and the car, where no one would be likely to hear them. She must want privacy.

Sure enough, a moment later Daphne turned to her

granddaughter. "I wanted to give you this." She handed Zoe a hardbound, dark brown leather book. "This was your grandfather's. I knew Ray wanted to give it to you or Hannah, so I figured you, since you appreciate the culture of old books. And I personally think that you'll empathize with this book better than Hannah."

"Oh… thank you very much. I will take good care of it." Zoe hugged the book close to her.

The feel of the book was different from other classics she had held. It was heavy, but not just weight-wise. There was something about it. As she held it, Zoe felt emotions were flowing from it into her. Feelings like pain, love and joy were definitely a part of this book.

She wasn't sure what this book was, but she felt that it had been very personal to her grandfather, so she knew she would read it for that reason alone. But her curiosity was alert to all the peculiarities about the book, too. Suddenly she could hardly wait until she was alone and could open it.

She hugged her Gran once more and then stepped back as Gran made her way to the car. Daphne got into the passenger seat as Zoe walked back to the house. Once she reached the front door, she turned and waved to her grandmas as they drove away.

She came back into the house just as it was time for

the kids and teens to get ready for bed.

The bathroom was crowded with Hannah, Tilly, all of the boys and Pammy, all trying to brush their teeth at the same time. The boys eventually gave up and went into the kitchen and tried to spit out the toothpaste in there.

"You boys get out of here, with your mouths full of toothpaste. Go back in the bathroom. Cole, don't talk with your mouth full!" Aunt Naomi hollered from the kitchen.

Zoe, in her pajamas, stood in the living room, looking out the glass sliding doors.

"Go on, get outta here." Martha said playfully motioning for the boys to go. The boys walked up the stairs behind Hannah and headed into their room.

"Come on." Hannah called down to Zoe, then headed into Tilly and Pammy's room. Zoe finished brushing her teeth and went upstairs to join Hannah, Tilly and Pammy. Zoe set out her sleeping bag next to Pammy's bed, like Hannah had set hers out next to Tilly's bed.

When everyone was either in bed or in their sleeping bag, Zoe pulled out the book her Gran had given her. Running her fingers over the cover, almost immediately she felt that strange transfer of emotion.

She wanted to open the book, to explore the pages, but Tilly had already turned out the light and her book light was packed away.

Tomorrow was another day. She could find time then maybe. With that in mind, she tucked the book away and scooted down into her sleeping bag.

Tomorrow was the day they would leave New York and head to Shadowhill. A new place to live. A new town. New people they would meet. Hopefully, some of those people would be friends.

Hopefully.

Zoe woke up to the smell of bacon, pancakes and maple syrup filling her nose. Today was the day... the day she left the city life behind her, no more unending sirens through the night, no more car accidents twice a week, no more neighbors yelling at each other at 3:00 a.m. Instead, she would be entering a small town world... crickets at sunset, peace filled evenings, birds chirping in the morning, everyone knowing everybody.

But there was something else that Zoe wanted...

Yes, she had been craving life in a small town, but there was something else—a secret—that she didn't tell anyone. If she told anyone, they'd call her mad—she probably was—but this secret was the very reason she closed herself off with books. And it was yet another reason why she didn't fit in with the kids her age.

"Wake up, Zoe." Pammy had come back into the room when Zoe wasn't looking and was now jumping on Zoe's sleeping bag.

"Good morning Pammy." Zoe said, turning to lay on her back and sitting up to face her young, energetic cousin.

If there was anything a person needed to know about Zoe, it would be that she is not a morning person, but somehow she found a way to present a polite manner.

"Daddy's cooking breakfast." Pammy said, bouncing up and down on her cousin's legs.

Zoe rubbed the sleep out of her eyes and sighed. She was tired, but she wasn't gonna say no to Pammy. "Well then, we don't want that to go to waste, do we?" Zoe teased.

The girls laughed as Zoe climbed out of her sleeping bag. She grabbed Pammy's hand as they left the bedroom, then they raced downstairs to the living room.

Pammy stopped and dropped onto the floor to pet Pumpkin.

In the dining room, Hannah was setting the table.

"Mommy?" Pammy called.

A minute later, Aunt Naomi popped her head out of the kitchen. "Yes?"

"Can me and Zoe have a picnic in here, as a special treat before they leave?" Pammy pleaded.

"Yes sweetie, you and Zoe can have a picnic." Aunt Naomi smiled at her daughter.

Zoe looked over at her cousin and she could see Pammy's face light up in a smile just before she turned and ran back up the stairs. Zoe looked back to Aunt Naomi, who smiled at her, before disappearing back into the kitchen.

Pammy came back with a huge blanket in her arms. "We're gonna have a picnic." Pammy dropped the blanket in a clump on the floor, covering Pumpkin.

A moment later, Pumpkin barked, then came out from under the blanket and ran into the dining room. Zoe knelt down and started spreading it out. Pammy helped, imitating what Zoe was doing.

Once it was spread out, they sat down on the blanket, Zoe fought against the tired feeling that crept into her body... the kind that comes when you feel wrapped up in a soft, comfortable blanket. It didn't help that Pammy laid down on the blanket. And then Pumpkin came back into the room, walked over to the blanket and laid down with her head and front paws on the blanket.

Zoe watched Pammy petting Pumpkin, and a feeling of peace swept over her. This moment seemed to stretch into a thousand moments, never to be lived in again. Zoe didn't know why this moment seemed to go on forever, but there was a restful peace in watching her cousin pet her sister's dog.

Suddenly, Zoe had a feeling that something great was about to happen... something was going to happen that would change her life, and the life of her family. And there would be no turning back...

It didn't scare Zoe. It wasn't a scary feeling. The feeling was a little sad, but also hopeful. Whatever was coming, Zoe somehow knew she would love it. Maybe it would finally be a step into the life she'd always wanted.

And that moment, that seemed to go on forever... it unexpectedly ended as quickly as it had come.

Just then, Hannah walked into the living room.

Pammy looked up at her cousin and asked, "Why are you still wearing such dark colors? I don't understand that. Other colors are so much prettier."

Hannah looked at Pammy, with eyes full of pain. A feeling of sympathy overtook Zoe as she looked at her sister, who had endured so much pain.

Hannah didn't say a word to anyone. She just walked away.

Pammy was too young to understand this now. She turned to Zoe. "Did I say something bad?"

"I'll explain this to you when you're older, sweetie." Zoe said, still looking at the floor where her sister had stood just a moment ago.

She understood that it hadn't been a long time since their grandfather passed, but Zoe feared that Hannah was so closed up, that she wouldn't ever open back up.

They had been so close.

After breakfast Hannah, Zoe, Ryan and Martha got dressed, gathered their stuff and got ready to leave. Uncle Darryl put their bags in Martha's car just as Daphne and Lorena arrived to bid the Autumns farewell.

Zoe leaned down and hugged Pammy.

"I wish time would freeze this moment so I could relive it over and over." Zoe said, thinking over what had happened just an hour ago, but this time it didn't stretch the moment into a thousand.

"So that you could be sad that someone you love is leaving?" Pammy asked her.

"No, so that I could have a moment of happiness, because when I leave, time will keep going and I'm gonna have to ride in a car with my brother all the way to Connecticut." Zoe said.

"Yeah, boys are no fun in a car." Pammy laughed. She would know Zoe's pain when it came to annoying brothers... and she had two of them.

Zoe pulled away, but remained at her eye level. "I love you, cousin."

Zoe wiped a tear from Pammy's cheek, then kissed her on her head. "I'll see you at my birthday party."

"See ya." Pammy said, then tackled Zoe for one last

hug.

After everyone else had been hugged and kissed, and Ryan, Hannah and Martha were finally in the car, Zoe gave Tilly another hug. She may be a little bit difficult at times, but they were cousins, after all. Family tended to love each other in spite of it all. Then Zoe hugged her uncle. Then Aunt Naomi. And her two grandmas. And then she tousled Henry and Cole's hair and gave Pammy another quick hug with a kiss on the cheek and then got in the car and waved, as Martha pulled out of the driveway and away from the house.

And then they were on their way.

Four people with four very different outlooks for what lay ahead.

To Martha it was a fresh start. To Ryan it wasn't a choice he would make, leaving his friends and school, to a place he didn't know and would probably dislike. To Hannah it was like a ghost of a feeling. She didn't think about or trust her feelings much these days, except for the powerful ones... the ones that really impacted her soul.

She honestly didn't know how she felt about moving to Shadowhill, she liked that her grandfather had lived there and now so would she, but she still felt unsure.

To Zoe, it was a new opportunity to live the life she'd

always wanted. She hoped that in this small town she would find a life that she could call hers, a life that no one had lived before, doing things no one else had done before.

She wished for a life of adventure.

SHADOWHILL

GOING HOME

The drive probably only seemed long because of the annoying little brother in the back seat...

Ryan fidgeted in his seat. Then he kept asking how much longer until they got to where they were going. He drove them all crazy.

Zoe tried to keep smiling for her mom, but every once in a while she would have to roll her eyes. Hannah put in both of her headphones and paid no mind to her family. Zoe tried not to mind, she was going through a lot and

Hannah wasn't really in any shape to be pleasant.

Several times during the trip, their mom pulled into a gas station or a rest stop... and they all pretty much went the same way.

"Everyone out, to stretch your legs." Martha would call out. "Take this opportunity to go to the bathroom. We're not stopping again for awhile."

Hannah would clip the leash on Pumpkin, so she could walk around and stretch her legs, too. Then Hannah would open the car door and let Pumpkin jump out. Usually Hannah would be yanked out of the car and pulled along by Pumpkin, who was delighted to be free to run a bit.

"Slow down." Hannah would yell, trying to keep up with Pumpkin, who was paying no attention to her, as she searched and sniffed for a spot on the ground to do her business.

Zoe and Ryan would go off to the bathrooms, then they would walk around outside at the rest stops, or walk along the aisles in convenience stores while their mom was at the gas pump, filling the fuel tank. After paying for the fuel, Mom would usually visit the bathroom, too.

Once Pumpkin had done her business and gotten some of her energy out, Hannah would bring her back to the car and take her turn in the bathroom.

When they were all back outside, their mom would call out, "Come on, everyone. Time to go."

Hannah and Zoe would get back in the car right away. Ryan would get in, whining that he didn't want to be in the car anymore. Then mom would get back in and start driving.

"Are we there yet?" Ryan asked for the eighteenth time.

Zoe had kept track to see just how many times her brother could ask.

"We're almost to the welcome sign, sweetie." Martha replied, with a sigh.

Hannah removed her headphones when her mother answered, but continued to stare out her window.

"I'm excited to be moving into grandpa's old house." Zoe noted.

"Me too. Did you know that I've only seen it the one

time?" Martha said.

"Really?" Zoe asked.

"Yep. Your grandfather lived here while he was growing up. Then he moved away for awhile. At some point he moved back. After a death in the family, he moved to New York. And that's where he met my mother."

Martha stopped a moment to take a sip of her soda. "I've only seen it the one time his lawyer took me through... about a month ago."

"What about you, Hannah?" Zoe asked. "Are you excited about moving into grandpa's old house?"

"Yes." Hannah said in a less than enthusiastic tone.

This dimmed Zoe's spirit for only a few seconds.

A few minutes later, with a smile on her face and a slightly relieved tone in her voice, Martha announced. "We've reached the town!"

Ryan cheered, "Yay!"

Zoe looked around, smiling, and Hannah... well, she just sighed.

"It's just a bunch of trees." Ryan said a minute later,

disappointment coloring his voice.

"This isn't what the entire town looks like, of course." Zoe tried to sway her strange-minded brother.

Hannah watched as they drove past trees and buildings. Just as they turned, she saw a sign that read *"Ridgedale Point – next left"*.

Hannah felt something inside of her jump for joy, almost like she had returned home, although she had never been there in her entire life. They had never visited or spent time there. Grandpa had lived in New York for as long as she could remember. So Hannah shook away the feeling and tried not to worry about it.

On Hazel Day Lane they passed a cemetery, a gas station, a synagogue, a bus station, a dance studio and a store that looked kind of interesting. At the end of Hazel Day Lane, they turned right onto a roundabout and then turned right on Main Street. Here they saw restaurants and more businesses.

They passed Northside Street on the left and at the end of Main Street they turned right onto Dreaming Tree Lane. As far as they could see, there was one long, deep forest of trees on the left.

They watched the right side, looking for their grandfather's home. Sunset Road was almost hidden in the woods on the right, then more woodland until they went past one lone house, then more of the forest for awhile.

They were excited to pass the entrance to a neighborhood, but it was mostly hidden by more woods. Eventually they stopped in front of a small house on the right.

Hannah leaned over to glance at it. "Is this it?"

Her mom didn't answer. Instead, she headed toward a driveway just ahead on the left. She stopped the car at the entrance of a gravel driveway. "This is it."

"Oh wow! This is it?" Hannah asked, looking over at a mansion. It was beautiful! It looked simple, yet elegant. A warm feeling began to spread over her.

"Yes!" Martha answered.

"Oh..." Hannah said quietly, the warm feeling growing, getting stronger. Finally, after moving from place to place all her life... from San Diego to Myrtle Beach, then to New Orleans, then to Nashville, and on to Manhattan. Now, arriving in Shadowhill, Connecticut, Hannah finally felt like she was home.

Martha turned onto the driveway and the three kids looked at their new home.

To Ryan, it was just another place that he was being dragged to. To Zoe, it was another place where she could unlock untold and visionary secrets. But to Hannah… it was a place that she could rest well at the end of the day—a safe place—a place she could hide from the rest of the world.

Home.

"There it is!" Martha said.

"It's hideous." Ryan said in disgust.

Hannah didn't say anything. She wanted to tell him that he was wrong, but she couldn't take her eyes off of how beautiful it was.

"That's your opinion, Ryan. It's beautiful." Zoe spoke for herself and Hannah.

Hannah smiled weakly, it was different between them now, than it had been while they were growing up. They had been two peas in a pod. But when they'd moved to New York, Hannah had changed—about the time she'd met Maggie…

Hannah was somewhat aware of this but didn't really ever talk about it. A slight twinge of guilt washed over her... Zoe never had found friends in real life. In books maybe, but not real life. Hannah worried that maybe she should have been there for her sister a little more, instead of chasing after popularity with Maggie.

They pulled up in front of the house and everyone piled out of the car.

"Guys, grab some of your stuff and go pick out your room. You can have whichever one you want." Martha said.

Hannah grabbed her bag next to her seat, her guitar case, and Pumpkin's leash and headed toward the house.

Ryan grabbed his bag and ran in ahead of everyone.

Zoe grabbed her air mattress and her large bag and walked in with Hannah side by side.

The double front doors were beautiful. They were made of dark wood with metal plating around the edges. The metal was engraved with Celtic symbols. And each door was outfitted with a small, brass plate with a heart engraved on it. The brass door knocker, when it tapped the middle of the heart, would echo throughout the house.

The double doors swung open easily. No one had lived here in a while, but someone had clearly been taking care of everything.

The inside was extraordinary. The marble floor had beautiful designs and the staircase in front of the entrance was covered in thick, red carpeting. And off to each side were rooms and hallways leading to other rooms. The house looked like it must have been built in the late eighteenth or early nineteenth century, but someone had obviously updated some of the rooms.

"It's the same on the inside." Ryan said, breaking the silence.

"It's beautiful, Ryan." Hannah said in awe.

"Are you kidding?" Ryan said, drawing Hannah's attention.

"What do you mean by that?"

"Well, look at all the cobwebs and drapes covering some of the windows." Ryan replied.

Hannah looked around again. Now she noticed the cobwebs and drapes covering some windows, and the floor was dusty. "It's still beautiful to me."

"Agreed." Zoe said.

"Whatever." Ryan said as he walked away and ran up the stairs. "Freaks." Ryan added softly as he ran up the stairs

Zoe rolled her eyes.

Hannah put her hand on her chest where her heart was. It was a strange feeling, that had happened before, just after her grandfather passed. This feeling was warm and tingly, but it was hard for Hannah to describe even to herself.

All she knew was that she'd felt this warm, tingly sensation and then a minute later she'd crushed a doorknob... and even then, she'd suspected that the feeling had something to do with her strength going wacky.

Oh no, what next?

"You ok?" Zoe asked.

Hannah had momentarily forgotten that her sister was next to her. "Yeah, totally." She took her hand away from her heart and smiled.

But the smile faded as quickly as it came, for only a few seconds passed where Hannah forgot her recent horrors, where she was determined to hide her secrets.

"Well, even if it was only for a few seconds, it was nice

to see a smile." Zoe walked across the marble floor and headed up the stairs to look for her new room.

When Hannah was able to focus again on herself and not her sister, she realized that the floor didn't look as dusty as before. That was strange. Maybe she was seeing things differently because she finally felt like she was home. Either way, she shrugged and tried to let it go for the moment. She headed for the stairs, slowly following Zoe and Ryan, looking around as she went.

When she got to the top, she looked back where she'd just come from. Now, it looked almost perfectly clean, no sign of their footprints anywhere... which was weird.

She had no way to explain it.

"Must be the distance." Hannah said to herself as she turned and headed down the hall on one side, trying to forget the oddity with the floors and searching for a bedroom at the same time.

Hannah walked down a very long hall, with multiple doors on either side. When she reached the end of that hall, she turned left and kept walking. This was a longer hall that connected to other halls. She kept going. At the end, she turned left again and walked down a long hall of even more rooms.

When Hannah reached the end of that hall, she looked

to her right and saw an ordinary wood door that somehow seemed more interesting to her. She opened the door and went in.

The room seemed like her kind of room, with wood floors. The wall that faced the doorway had two large windows that almost covered the wall. There was also a door that led to a balcony that, when she went over and looked out of the glass on the door, she saw that it overlooked the cemetery next to the house. There was also a large walk-in closet.

Hannah put her bag down by the closet door, let go of Pumpkin's leash and then left, heading back out to the car to get her air mattress.

Once she got back to the car, she got her air mattress and her other bag and headed back to her chosen room. Once she was back in her room, she dropped her other bag next to the first, rolled out the air mattress, and started the pump to inflate it.

Once that was done, she started looking through her bags. She pulled out some of her favorite knick-knacks, a doll and a couple of dog toys for Pumpkin. When she pulled out the metallic chess piece, a white Queen that her grandfather had given to her on the day he died, a tear slipped down her cheek.

He had just gotten back from an out of town trip and

he'd stopped by for a visit. He'd told her when he arrived that he couldn't stay long. But while he was there, he'd given her the white Queen chess piece.

Hannah remembered asking him "Why a white Queen?"

He'd simply replied "White has only one rule that Black does not, that makes them unique to Black... Never let anyone ever tell you that unique is bad."

At this memory, more tears came. What had come next was painful... almost too painful to think about. Hannah had begged her grandfather to stay a little while longer, but he'd had to leave to run an errand.

He hadn't gotten the chance. A truck had hit his car and he'd been rushed to the hospital. He spent several hours there, but had succumbed to a heart attack. And that was that.

He was gone now.

Putting the chess piece back in her bag, she pushed the memories away. When she did, she saw what she had been looking for—a sign. It was made of wood, painted black and, on the front in neon teal letters was written simply "Hannah".

A small rope was tied through little holes on each end.

She looked through her bags until she found the small container of thumb tacks from her room, pulled one out and then went to her new door. When she had the sign where she wanted it, she pushed a thumb tack into the wood door. It went in much easier than she'd thought it would. She knocked her knuckles against the door, thinking maybe it was hollow or something. But the door sounded hard and definitely not hollow when she wrapped her fist against it.

Shrugging at the oddness of it, she hung her sign on the tack, sighed and stepped back to look at her handiwork. Looking at the sign, Hannah felt there was a chance that she would break into tears again, so she decided to go outside and explore to distract herself.

MYSTERY OF TRUTH OR FALSE

Walking through the mansion, Hannah noticed there was a certain something in the air. It almost seemed like the house was sad, but maybe cheering up because of new people being there. She couldn't help but wonder, was it happier just because of new people moving in? Or was it happier because Ray's family had finally returned?

Hannah looked around from wall to wall, ceiling to floor, her hands in her front pockets, slowly walking through the mansion. She came to the main staircase and slowly walked down them. The marble floor was definitely less dusty now, but the room itself was lighter, it seemed to be that someone had pulled the drapes off the windows. Maybe her mom. She was most likely cleaning as she went. Hannah knew the cobwebs alone would drive her crazy.

Since she really didn't want to go looking for her and bother her, she just quietly slipped out the front door.

She hadn't really focused on the outside when they'd first arrived. The house had been too mesmerizing. But now she could see that the outside was beautiful. The trees were changing colors. There was orange, yellow, and red in all of them. And the grass had fallen leaves spread across it, that crunched whenever a bunny or a squirrel bounded across.

Hannah looked to the driveway and saw a boy and a girl walking up the driveway. They were making their way to Hannah.

She slowly walked toward them. She didn't really feel like socializing, but these must be their new neighbors. Better to get it over with and go on with her day.

As they got closer, Hannah could make out more clearly what they looked like. The girl had long red hair and light green eyes. She wore a green, dark pink, and yellow striped shirt, blue jeans, and dark blue tennis shoes.

And the boy had black hair and brown eyes. He wore a green shirt, dark blue jeans, and black tennis shoes.

Each of them held a container with a lid on them.

"Bring on the parade of casseroles."

They stopped walking about two feet away from Hannah. The girl seemed nervous but excited.

"Hi, I'm Kiki Chase, and this is my friend Jack Palmer."

"I'm Hannah Autumn." Hannah responded.

"Nice to meet you, we just wanted to welcome you into our little town." Kiki spoke again.

"How did you know that we would be coming?" Hannah asked, knowing that they hadn't stopped to talk to anyone and their car didn't make it obvious.

"Oh it's been buzzing around town ever since that lawyer was here with a very nice lady. We've all been so excited for new people to come."

Hannah guessed that the lady in Kiki's story was her mom and the lawyer must have been her grandfather's lawyer.

"She's always liked this house, she's obsessed with houses that have a mysterious history." Jack spoke up.

"Just a little bit." Kiki said quietly. She looked shy, and maybe a little embarrassed by what Jack had told Hannah. In fact, she almost reminded Hannah of Zoe.

"So when she heard that someone was moving in, she saw this as an opportunity to get closer to the house."

"What do you mean, *mysterious history*?" Hannah asked.

"Your parents didn't tell you?" Kiki asked.

Hannah shook her head.

"Do you want to tell her or shall I?" Kiki asked Jack.

"You tell her, you tell it better." Jack answered Kiki.

"Thanks!" Kiki smiled, cleared her throat and began her tale.

"It all started in seventeen-nineteen. An ordinary man, named William Harris, lived here with his wife and their two kids. They all seemed pretty normal." She stopped a moment, but went on quickly.

"Well... William was a little odd." Jack rolled his eyes. Clearly, he had heard this story before.

"One night not long before Halloween, the family threw a party for the town... pretty much the whole town." She spread her hands wide on either side of her with an expression of awe, before going on.

"Almost everyone in town was there, dressed up in masquerade outfits. But when the clock struck 10:00 p.m., a woman dressed in black from head to toe, with a black mask walked into the mansion… Not a lot of people noticed her. She came in quietly, without making a fuss. The woman in black walked over to William's wife. She didn't greet her or thank her for allowing her into her home… Instead she lifted her up into the air, with her witch abilities and started choking her. It was then that everyone noticed them. They all backed away in fear, except for William. He rushed over to the woman in black and stopped her from hurting his wife." She stopped there for a few seconds, took a deep breath—and then started again.

"He had the woman in black burned at the stake, thinking that his family would be safe. But what he didn't know was that the woman survived." She paused again, for a slightly shorter pause.

"The stories go on and tell of how the woman in black would only come out at night... to get rid of all the people that had helped to persecute her. People were living in fear. Some moved away. Some moved far away. William feared for his family's safety, and he wanted to send them away, but his wife was determined to stay with him. They died a week later, leaving their children to be raised by their aunt and uncle."

One last pause. And then...

"And the woman in black was never seen again."

"That's horrible." It took her a second, but Hannah finally spoke.

"I know. And no one knows why the woman in black did what she did." Kiki added.

"That's so sad." Jack added.

"Especially for their children." Kiki added sadly.

"You do remember that it's just a story, right? Like all the other stories around here, vampires and ghosts are just stories." Jack sounded so sure. There was no hint of doubt in his voice. This was a person who did not believe in the supernatural.

"So do you believe in stuff, like vampires and ghosts?" Hannah asked Kiki.

"Heck no, it's impossible for someone to be undead or to be on this earth after dying." Jack spoke before Kiki could answer.

Kiki's head immediately turned toward him with an annoyed look. Hannah had a feeling that Jack got that a lot.

Hannah tried not to let her reaction show on her face... trying instead to make it seem like she was just ignoring him.

Kiki turned back to Hannah, her face relaxed now. "I personally…" Kiki gave Jack a look, then looked back at Hannah. "Believe in the possibility of vampires, ghosts and witches."

Kiki added. "The world just seems too big a place to be that small."

Hannah chuckled.

"Something funny?" Kiki asked.

"No, it's just that you sounded like my sister. She says slightly strange things in that same…" She paused a second, weighing her next words carefully. She had just met these people. On the other hand, after that story, did she care of they were offended or not? "… odd way."

"Oh." Kiki smiled.

"Would you like to come in?" Hannah asked.

"Oh yes, I'd love to. I've always wanted to see the

house up close, but something always prevented me from it."

This statement piqued Hannah's curiosity, but she didn't want to press someone she had just met.

"Yeah. Sure, let's go in." Jack said.

Hannah turned to walk toward the house, a tiny bit weirded out by their reactions and how different they were. She told herself that if she couldn't handle them, she'd just leave them to Zoe.

"Oh my goodness!" Kiki exclaimed as soon as she stepped through the front door. Jack remained silent.

"Yeah, It's amazing." Hannah agreed, looking around at the majesty of her new home.

"You are so lucky to be living here. What I would give to live here." Kiki said. "How did you come to live here? It must have cost a fortune."

"Well, I guess it did whenever it was built. I actually inherited it from my grandfather. He passed a few months ago." Hannah answered, looking down as the emotions threatened to swamp her.

"I am so, so, so sorry." Kiki said.

Hannah looked back up in surprise. She could tell

from her voice that she was being more sincere than anyone in New York had ever been when they'd said that to her.

"Thank you." She managed a small smile. "My grandfather grew up here and then moved away for a time. Then he moved back, but moved away again after there was a death in the family. That was when he moved to New York."

Kiki opened her mouth to say something, but was interrupted by Hannah's mom.

"Hello, I'm Hannah's mom, Martha Autumn."

She was panting a little between breaths. She must have been in another room cleaning or tidying up.

"Mom, this is Kiki Chase and Jack..." Hannah paused, forgetting Jack's last name. She racked her brain trying to remember, but she just couldn't.

"Palmer." Jack jumped in, understanding her look. "A lot of people forget my last name, so don't sweat it."

Martha smiled as she shook Kiki and Jack's hands.

"Oh! Speaking of forgetting. Before I forget, I made this for you, as sort of a welcoming present." Kiki opened the lid on her container to reveal brownies. "Peanut butter chocolate fudge brownies. They're kinda my specialty." She nudged Jack.

"Oh, mine is a simple…"

"But delicious…" Kiki interrupted him.

"…chicken casserole." Jack said as he handed over his container.

"Thank you." Martha took both containers.

"Of course." Kiki said in her bubbly, excited way. "The entire town has been excited about your family coming, so we've all been baking stuff—getting ready to welcome you to our town."

She glanced down at her watch, then looked back up at Hannah, but then back down to her watch again. Her head shot straight up, her eyes wide as quarters. "Oh crap." She looked at Jack.

"What?" Jack asked.

"Is there a problem?" Hannah asked.

"No. Not a problem—exactly. I just have to get home. My mom wants me home early." She explained. "Nothing serious."

"Is it because your grandma is staying for the week?" Jack asked.

"Yes." Kiki answered, it almost sounded like she loathed admitting it. But then her voice was back to bubbly and excited. "Well, it was a pleasure meeting you."

"Yeah, maybe we could show you around, once you get settled in." Jack added.

He seemed excited at the idea and Hannah didn't show it, but she was actually getting a happy feeling about the idea of hanging out with the two of them.

"Yeah, the moving truck comes tomorrow, so once we get settled, I'll give you a call." Hannah said.

"Then I'll give you our numbers!" Kiki said as she pulled out a little card with writing on it.

"Here you go, it has both our numbers so you can call whoever!" Kiki said as she gave Hannah the card, smiling her big, enthusiastic smile the entire time.

For some reason, despite her bubbly attitude, Hannah got the feeling maybe she didn't have a lot of friends. Though she genuinely seemed to want to spend more time with Hannah — which was such a refreshing change from the phonies in New York.

She was being nice... not because of Hannah's hairstyle... *which is a mess, by the way...* or because of her outfit... *which is just plain clothes in dark colors...* but because she wanted to really spend time with her to get to know her. It was a really nice feeling — to know that she already had a couple of people who wanted to spend time with her.

"Well, I'll see ya." Hannah said as she walked them to the door.

"Oh yeah! Soon!" Kiki bubbled. "And thanks for letting me come in and see your house."

She seemed particularly grateful for that. It was kinda refreshing for Hannah — to see the two of them just being who they were. In New York, everyone was trying to be someone else, copy someone else. But here Kiki and Jack seem to just be themselves, no front, no phony, just them.

"You're welcome!" Hannah was surprised at how she was looking forward to seeing them again as she closed the door.

"Good to know that we have nice neighbors."

"Yeah, it is." Hannah stood there a few seconds, watching them walk down the long driveway. "Hey Mom, I think I'm going to go explore outside some."

"Sure thing, honey. Just be back inside in time for dinner."

"Thanks, Mom. I will." Hannah opened the door, but before she stepped out, her mother called to her.

"I'll just be tidying up in some of the rooms, in case you need me."

"Kay." Hannah answered. She watched her mom head back down the hall she had emerged from earlier. When she was gone, Hannah turned back and walked out the open door, closing it tight behind her.

She walked around the right side of the mansion and kept going toward the back of the impressively large building. Past the small cemetery, there was a small open field and then it dropped off.

Hannah walked over to the cliff and looked down. It was a deep drop off, but below was what looked like a lake with a large creek at the far end providing drainage. It wound away, disappearing in the distance. On the nearer end, behind or beside the cemetery—she wasn't sure of her exact orientation to North or South, and the sun was currently hiding behind thick clouds in the sky.

It was a peaceful place, the sort of place someone could sit and look out to the horizon. The sound of their thoughts would easily be drowned out by the water, while they enjoyed the view.

Breathing in the clean air and that wonderful smell

that seemed to always be present around a lake or a river, she turned her back to the cliff, and looked at the cemetery... and felt intrigued.

It had a stone wall pretty much all around it that reached Hannah's waist as she walked closer to it. On top of that wall, there were iron poles about ten or twelve inches tall that ended in sharp spikes.

"Hmm." Reaching the entrance, Hannah opened the small metal gate and walked in.

It looked like any other cemetery she had been in, but there was something about this one. It felt... different somehow.

She started walking through the cemetery, following the winding stone path that followed a strange path through the freshly mown grass and tombstones, when something on one of the tombstones caught her eye. She walked over to it and looked closer, trying to see what it was that had caught her eye.

Hannah didn't know why this piqued her interest. She knew "Matthews" was her mom's maiden name. Maybe that was it? Wasn't Matthews a pretty common name? Not like Autumn. She wouldn't find anyone in here with that last name, she was pretty sure.

After another minute, Hannah moved away from the tombstone and ventured closer to the forest.

It had seemed like a long way to go, but Hannah reached the end of the cemetery, which was the beginning of the forest, fairly quickly. The stone wall was here too, but it was almost as if it was being swallowed up by the forest. In some places, the trees had taken over completely. In others, they were simply hanging low over the wall, hiding it from view.

She looked back to the mansion, wondering if she should go any further. A feeling deep down told her to go. Hannah shrugged and walked toward the wall. As she got closer, she saw that there was a gate there too.

Vines had wound up all around it from either side, but this gate was different from the one she had walked through to get into the cemetery. That one had been a single gate that swung open. This was a double set of gates that opened in the middle.

She pushed, half-expecting the vines to keep her from moving either side, but they swung open easily. The vines were wrapped tightly, but not stopping the movement of the hinges one bit.

Hannah walked from the cemetery to the forest, blinking a little at the sudden change in light. The trees had closed in, but she could still see. The light was simply different. She walked through the winding path that led deeply into the forest. Every now and then, a leaf or two would drop. And the leaves on the ground crunched when she walked on them.

After some time, Hannah came to an open area in the forest. There was a stone bench with fluffy, red pillows propped on it in the clearing. The bench sat under a fully grown weeping willow.

Intrigued, she walked over to the bench and ran her fingers over the pillows. Surprisingly, they almost felt as soft as Pumpkin's fur. Hannah sat down on the bench and leaned into the soft pillow. Suddenly Hannah felt very tired, so she laid her head down on the pillow and tucked her legs up on the bench.

I'll just rest my eyes for a minute...

Then she closed her eyes.

EXPLORATION APLENTY

Zoe slowly walked down the hall that was beyond the main staircase. She ate tortilla chips that were covered in a spicy nacho cheese flavored powder. The few times when she reached the end of a hall, she turned left, but then she came to a hall where she turned right.

When she reached another hall on the left, she turned. Then she walked until she reached a set of stairs—also on her left.

Zoe stared at the stairs, curious about where they

went. When she decided to go up the stairs, she took hold of her bag of chips and ran the other hand along the railing as she climbed the stairs.

When she reached the top of the stairs she looked around at the new floor. She wondered just how much of the mansion her mother had explored when she'd come with her grandfather's lawyer. Had she come inside at all? If they had, how far had they come? Had anyone even been up here since her grandfather's leaving? If not, she could be the first one up here in the last sixty years.

A lone, dusty coffee table sat in the middle of the large room before her. This floor, like the entire house, felt like an age that had been forgotten to the world. But sometimes when she looked at a wall or a piece of art, it was almost like the house was smiling at her. People might call her crazy, but she wasn't convinced that was actually a bad thing...

In fact, she typically considered it an insult if you called her sane—or normal.

As she walked deeper into the large room, she looked all around. To her right, there was a hallway leading past the stairs and going deeper into the mansion. On her left, there was a large area beyond the stairs and then what looked like a closet next to them. Beyond that, there were a couple more hallways leading away from the area.

It all seemed like a maze at first, but as Zoe stood there soaking up the air, it felt more and more familiar. More like home. She turned to the stairs that led up, the ones next to the stairs she had just come up, and began to climb them, too.

"Zoe."

She turned partly back to the whispering voice behind her, keeping her hand on the handrail. There was no one there. She searched the room for evidence of a person or something... anything... that could explain someone calling her name.

Nothing. No one.

"Hello?" Zoe inquired, but no voice returned.

There was no sound in the room, except the sound of Zoe's beating heart. Even though her curiosity was blazing, wondering about the voice, it was burning even more to see the next floor, so she turned away from the room and started climbing the stairs again. At the landing, there was a door.

She slowly reached for the door knob. Her fingers wrapped around the cold, icy door knob. Zoe twisted the knob and the door opened with a subtle creak.

She looked inside the room. It was pitch black. She

waited a few seconds, but when her eyes didn't adjust to the darkness, she pulled out her phone and turned on the flashlight.

Armed with her phone's bright flashlight, she walked into the dark room. Unlike the rest of the mansion, this room had a stone floor. Zoe's feet were bare and the floor felt positively icy against the bottom of her feet. It didn't take more than a step or two before the cold affected more than her feet. Pretty soon, her whole body felt cold. She shivered with it.

There was a wall ahead of her and nothing to her left. So, she turned right and found a corner. She followed it around to the right and then again when it kept turning. When it turned to the left, she kept going—into an even bigger, darker room. When she shined her flashlight around, she could see that all of the windows were covered with thick, heavy curtains that let in no light whatsoever.

When she took a step into the room, her feet left the stone floor behind and she was now walking on smooth, but cold hardwood. This cold didn't bother her though. In a way, it comforted her. It was like being cold and wrapped up in a comfortable blanket or her favorite sweater—which was something she dearly loved.

Zoe walked further into the room and realized it was

the attic. After a few minutes, her eyes began to adjust to the dim light that must be coming from somewhere—and, with the help of her flashlight, she looked further. The room was immense and filled with dust. The familiar smell of slightly musty, old books filled her nose.

Now that was a smell she could be comfortable with. There was nothing quite like the smell of old books. Whether they had been sitting in an attic for years or a musty old library, there was just something about the smell that made her feel right at home.

Like the rest of the house, the attic had obviously not been touched in many, many years. Decades upon decades... Dust swirled in the air and covered everything in the attic, but she felt at home.

As she explored, she found boxes upon boxes of books. There were old wooden horses that looked as if lots of children had played on them. There were shelves with knick knacks that were practically unrecognizable under the layers of dust.

But where to start?

Zoe decided to look in a box. Any box. She looked around, and a box not far from where she stood caught her eye.

She walked over, scanned the box with her flash light,

then placed the bag of chips on a box beside the box in front of her, then she licked her fingers clean, and wiped her hand on the back on her thigh.

Zoe opened the box carefully and pulled out layers of tissue paper, and then a tiny doll. It was obviously sewn by hand. It had no face. It wore a faded dress that might have once been dark blue. Its empty face, arms and legs were faded and yellowed with age. Faded red yarn was sewn on top of its head for hair. She looked down at the doll. This was obviously beloved, treasured, a source of hope, passed down through generations—carefully and painstakingly wrapped and packed away.

An image flashed into Zoe's mind, a girl about Hannah's age. She had a sweet face, blonde hair and blue eyes. The girl's face flashed into Zoe's mind and then it was gone.

Zoe smiled a little at the image in her mind. The girl looked a little familiar. She must have remembered the face from some of the old photo albums her grandfather kept at his house in New York. Carefully, she put the doll on the box on the other side of the open box—and then reached into the box again.

This time, she pulled out a book. It's cover was leather. It looked faded in places, but it was a brown leather that had darkened with age. The spine looked like it was actually sewn together with strands of leather—and the book was tied closed with another strand of dark brown leather.

She gently pulled on the knot that tied the book closed. The knot resisted at first, stubbornly refusing to budge. And then when Zoe actually stopped trying to untie it, it came undone.

Carefully, Zoe opened the book. The pages were a type of handmade pulp paper she had seen in some of the older books on display in the New York library, but they had been behind glass. She'd never been able to touch those. The texture was surprisingly smooth... probably worn smooth from handling and age. They were much less yellowed with age than she'd expected.

She slowly turned the pages. The writing on those pages was a language she did not recognize, the only written words that Zoe recognized were names. Peter. Roxanne. Nothing else.

She flipped through the pages almost halfway through the book. It was really old. Maybe it was written in an archaic dialect. And it wasn't like she knew all of them... only a little bit of a few. Maybe her phone or the internet would help.

She laid the pages out and tried taking a picture of the words, but the image came out all blurry, so fuzzy it was unreadable. It was awfully dark in the attic.

The mystery of the book would have to wait until she had more time to explore. She could try again after she'd found a light switch.

After putting away the mysterious book, Zoe picked up a blanket that lay beside the other books in the box. It had picked up the smell of the books it was packed with. She scrunched the blanket up in her fingers and then rubbed it gently against her arm. It was surprisingly soft, although a little bit musty.

She gently folded the blanket and laid it aside with the other books she had found. She wanted to turn her attention to the other boxes, but it was dark and she'd been wandering the house for a long time. If she didn't get back to where she could hear if someone yelled for her, they might start to worry if they did call out.

The books and blanket and doll, she carefully repacked in the box. The book was probably only in such good shape because of being packed away—and she didn't want to do anything that would mess that preservation up. If she ever wanted to look at them again, she would know where to find them.

Zoe walked quickly to her new room. Nostalgia had taken hold of her up in the attic and she felt the need to smell something from her childhood. Practically flying through her bedroom door, she rushed over to a box that she had brought up to her new room soon after she'd chosen it.

This box was not taped up. She hadn't want to tape the box up for the move, because it wouldn't be in a moving truck, but would be moving with them in the car and she'd wanted to be able to pull her stuff out of it and hold it if nostalgia spoke up in the seemingly long car ride with a pesky little brother and a nearly catatonic older sister.

Zoe opened the flaps of the box and pulled out a yellow, pink, teal and sky blue knitted blanket. It was her baby blanket. It was an heirloom, though she wasn't sure from whom... probably one of her grandmothers or a distant cousin.

Zoe asked her mother on occasion who that blanket had belonged to, but her mother would grow quiet and change the subject and depending on her mood, she would occasionally send Zoe to her room when she'd ask —almost as if it pained her mother to think of the blanket's origin.

Zoe had wondered at times if it was her father's, but he had always been so distant with her, she doubted that she could feel connected to anything he'd owned. She couldn't explain it, but she always felt a deep connection to the blanket. She kept it close so that she could one day cradle her own child in it.

And even though Zoe didn't know who her blanket had belonged to before it had been hers, she deeply loved that blanket. Whenever she was feeling nostalgic and needed comforting, Zoe would pull out the blanket, lay on her bed and snuggle with the blanket wrapped around her and pressed against her nose.

This time she sat on her carpet stained floor and buried her nose in the blanket.

A baby's laugh rang through Zoe's ears. The sound was kinda comforting to her. *Telma mai stein terana* sung through her head, words she never heard before, she quirked her eyebrows and lifted her head. *Telma mai stein terana?*

What did that mean?

She often heard things like that, like it was in her head, yet she was hearing it through her ear, almost like an inner ear. She had often wondered if that was normal, if it happened to other people?

Or just to her?

She'd never really asked anyone. Something always stopped her. Almost like an instinct. Even though she really didn't understand it.

Zoe wrapped her baby blanket around her shoulders, stood and walked over to the glass doors that opened into her small balcony and opened them.

She stood in the doorway, the familiar scents and feel of her childhood blanket comforting her—while her future stared her in the face.

She scrunched her eyebrows a little when she saw a dark figure heading for the woods. When she looked closer, though, she could see the medium blonde hair—and she realized it was Hannah… Hannah was going into the woods, by way of the cemetery.

Zoe was shocked to realize that Hannah was walking through a cemetery. When her sister had started hanging out with the popular crowd, she'd found cemeteries vile and never stepped foot in one unless someone had died.

Zoe, on the other hand, wasn't exactly fascinated by cemeteries, but she didn't freak out about them like some people did. However, whenever she'd been in a cemetery, she would never do anything to dishonor those who had passed.

She watched her sister disappear into the forest and then took a moment to look around at her new surroundings. There was so much to see. It would take a long time to explore everything. With that in mind, she turned around, set her blanket gently on her air mattress, and then left her room. She walked down the hallway her room was in. Then she went down the huge front stairs, turned right twice and then turned down the only hallway on the left.

She came to an intersection and went forward into a grand hall, complete with a glass chandelier. On the other side of the grand hall, another entrance turned into a hall.

She crossed the enormous room and then went down the connected hall, passing an open doorway that lead into a second kitchen and into another connected hall before she passed a door on her left.

She didn't stop though. Something told her to keep going, to turn here or there, to follow a certain path. It was the same sort of thing like with the music she didn't fully understand, so she didn't question it. She just followed. Right turn. Down the hall. Halfway down, turn right again.

She passed multiple doors on her right and only a couple on her left spread far apart. She reached the end of this hall and looked right and left, a quick turn to endless more rooms to her right, but only a few rooms to her left. She looked from side to side trying to decide which way to go, when she looked to the left once more, the smell of old books filled her nose.

Ahhhh.

That was what her mind had been telling her. Books!

She closed her eyes and inhaled deeply. Then she released her breath, feeling pleasantly relaxed and also strangely excited. She sighed in contentment at the familiar smell. Her decision made, she turned left. She went right past several rooms until she came to the last two rooms—right across from each other. She looked to her right. It wasn't instinct that told her this was the right door. It was her keen sense of smell that would always unerringly find books.

She reached over to the door, wrapped her hand around the knob and pulled open the door with an unexpectedly loud creek.

The room was enormous, so large, the corners were actually too dark to see into. There had to be hundreds of books on the walls... maybe thousands. The room stretched up into the 2nd floor, those walls filled with more bookshelves. They covered nearly every inch of the walls, except across from the main entrance where a large fireplace stood. It looked as if it had been well-used, but at the moment it soundlessly stood still, not a dance of light anywhere.

As Zoe entered the room, the smell of books filled her nose, causing her eyes to close as she focused on inhaling the sweet scent of the written word and that same familiar smell of books with an impressive amount of age.

She walked to the middle of the room and spun around while looking at the room. If she'd been wearing a skirt, it would have twirled.

Each wall had two rolling ladders on it, each one of them gathering dust in a different part of the library. A large carpet in the middle of the floor brought a feeling of old fashioned whimsy to the room. It looked coarse and a bit bunched up... likely from age and dust, but when she stepped onto it, the feel was not painful for her bare feet. She walked over to the left side of the room and climbed the spiral staircase there to the second floor.

Walking along the second floor, Zoe slowly brushed her fingers along the spines of the books, looking at the dust that had settled on the books and reading the spines at the same time.

She stopped and looked at a book on the shelf above her eye level. She would have to do some cleaning in here as soon as possible. The books needed to be free of dust — a substance which was the enemy of books. It would suck the moisture from the air and dry out the pages in books old and new.

Then she would be able to enjoy going through the shelves and reading as many of the books as she could. If her mom would let her, Zoe could have happily lived in the library.

With the books.

NIGHTFALL

Owls cooed from above. Frogs and crickets chirped. The fallen leaves rustled from the ground.

The sun was already hidden by the trees that covered the horizon. The monsters that hunt at night would be out, prowling the ground, waiting for the unaware innocent to slip up. To go down a dark alley. To go to the park alone. Run in the forest. Walk to their car in a deserted parking lot.

With no one to stop them, they got more and more

cocky. More daring. More determined. More brave. They attacked in more populated areas. They ventured where they once would not have dared.

But now that the Protector was finally here, Shadowhill would finally be saved from the unspeakable horrors that filled the hours of night.

Jared Callahan had watched the quiet mansion in Shadowhill for a long time. He had talked to some of the townspeople and he had learned that the house had been there for longer than Shadowhill had been a town.

A town where a large wooden sign was planted next to the walkway that led to town hall. The sign read *"Shadowhill."* in large script lettering. And underneath it read *"Established in 1833."* The next line read the coordinates "41.6525697, -72.3104332." At the very bottom was the last line, *"Population: 1,518"*.

When was the last time they updated that number?

There had to be more people than that in Shadowhill now...

And are they counting the monsters who also call our unsuspecting town home? Hmm... Probably not.

Jared watched the abandoned mansion as it's new residents entered, just as he'd been told they would. He had lurked from the forest just outside the cemetery, grateful that the trees hadn't shed every leaf. If they had, he would not have been able to hide from the young curious girl with brown hair as she looked past him and into the forest.

When she had gotten out of her mother's car, she'd looked at the forest. Jared had worried she might have seen him... from the curious tilt of her head. But after her brother raced into the house, her attention had been drawn back to the house.

Then, when her sister had come into the woods, Jared had hidden himself where she couldn't see him. Watching her piqued his interest, but now she had to get back to the house. Her sleeping put her in a very dangerous position.

She was vulnerable.

Jared turned away from the house and walked toward the willow tree. Not even eight steps into his stride, he stopped. He smelled the girl, but something else was close by. Jared's eyes widened and he sprinted forward, desperate to get to Hannah before the thing that foreign smell was coming from did.

He knew that smell. It was one of the very monsters that haunted the night. When the willow tree came into his line of sight, he saw that Hannah was still laying on the stone bench, but a monster was leaning over her.

Running faster now, he leapt in the air as the beast grasped her neck, Changing his form from human into wolf, he growled and attacked the beast. It fell, leaving Hannah alone, but it didn't run off. It struggled for a few meaningless seconds before Jared beheaded it. It turned to dust from underneath Jared. Taking only a few seconds to catch his breath before changing back to his human form, he turned back to Hannah.

She moaned sleepily on the ground in front of the stone bench. The monster must have still had hold of her when Jared had attacked.

He walked over to her, breathing deeply. He pressed against her right shoulder to make sure her neck was safe. At the sight of no blood, he sighed in relief.

Then he leaned down and rolled Hannah over and reached underneath her, his right arm under her shoulders and his left arm under her knees. He made sure that he had a good grip on her before turning away from the willow tree and heading back to the mansion.

A STRANGE AWAKENING

It was night... Hannah was walking through the mansion. The air was cold. All of the windows were open and the curtains moved like waves of water.

Hannah was on the second floor. She turned to the right, strolling down a hall, stopping at a door. When she reached out to jiggle the doorknob, it didn't budge. She turned to walk away, when she heard a noise from behind the door.

Hannah turned back to the door and reached for the

knob again, but before her hand could touch it, the door opened. On the other side was darkness. After a few eye squinting seconds passed, a dark silhouette figure appeared.

As she waited for her eyes to adjust to the darkness, she tried to make out who was there. Suddenly the person pounced on her, only he had fangs, claws, and deathly pale skin. He looked human—but otherworldly.

The stranger pulled Hannah to his side of the door, and they both went tumbling down the stairs. Hannah hit the floor hard! Pain shot up and down her back, her arms, legs, feet.

She closed her eyes for just a moment. She had to fight back. She had to get away. She had to stop the monster from hurting her... hurting her family... hurting her new neighbors...

When her eyes opened again, she sat up quickly, looking around. She was back in her room, on her air mattress.

It had all been a dream. Right? So how did I get here?

She put her hand on the right side of her neck. It was very painful, almost like her neck had gotten twisted up as she fell off of something.

She stood up and the room spun.

She fell against the wall and breathed deeply. Squeezing her eyes shut, she shook her head, trying to dispel the vertigo—and then she opened her eyes again. The room spun a bit, but started to slow—and finally came to a stop. She gently shook her head and blinked several times until her vision came into focus.

She took another deep breath, and pushed herself away from the wall, then stumbled to the door. When she opened her door, a light from down the hall shone into her eyes. She looked back at her room and realized that not a single light was on, but she could see just fine.

Though her curiosity was piqued, her second instinct pushed the curiosity down enough so she didn't just jump without thinking.

After another deep breath, she walked out of her room and closed the door behind her. The hall was eerily quiet, She glanced at her sister's door and then at the bottom of it. No light. Hannah figured her sister either wasn't there or she'd gone to bed.

Exactly how late is it?

Most nights, Zoe read well into the wee hours of the morning—especially when they didn't have to be up early for anything. But she'd clearly already gone to bed...

unless she wasn't in her room.

Hannah continued down the hall. There were no sounds from her sister's room, nor from her brother's or mother's rooms. She found herself worrying. Part of her hoped that the dream she'd had was just that—a dream. Nothing else.

But what if it hadn't been? What if it was something else?

She turned at the end of the hall and watched as she passed the few halls that lead only to a single window. At the end of this hall she turned right, then walked down the large open hall and headed down the grand front staircase.

She turned her head to the sound of voices to her left. Following the voices, she turned down a hall that turned left and followed until she came to a kitchen where her mother was preparing dinner.

A quick look through the window at the end of the hall where she was standing showed her that it was indeed dark outside. Yes, it was fall—and yes, the days had been getting shorter—but she hadn't thought she had been gone that long. That would mean she had slept on the stone bench she'd found for hours.

And how had she gotten back here afterwards?

Both were questions she had no answers for. So she let it go and watched her mother cook, thinking how lucky she was to have such a great cook for a mother.

A lot of people had moms who were either a menace in the kitchen or who had never cooked a day in their life. Martha Autumn was the exact opposite. She had been cooking since she was nine and she cooked better than a chef in any fancy restaurant from New York to San Diego.

The only thing Hannah didn't understand was how messy she was. Even with her years of experience, she was a disaster of a mess in the kitchen and it never improved, no matter how much she tried. But it didn't stay that way for long. Without fail, an hour after dinner, the kitchen would be spotless.

It was one of the reasons she and her sister and brother had learned to clean up after themselves in the kitchen... and pretty much everywhere else, too.

This kitchen was in the shape of a large rectangle. Martha was standing in front of the stove on the right wall, the sink was across from Hannah, with an island between Hannah and the sink—and a long counter between the sink and the refrigerator. There was a small counter and an oven next to Hannah, and then more counter space. At the far corner a round wood table with three wood chairs sat. They were obviously an old-fashioned, farmhouse style.

Hannah thought they must have been here already, because they hadn't brought such nice chairs. Her mother must have dusted them off because not a single inch of them held a speck of dust, even though they were obviously old. She figured they must be antiques. They were in great shape, even if they looked slightly faded from age.

"Hey Mom." Hannah rubbed some sleep from her right eye.

"Hi, honey." Martha looked over at Hannah as she stirred the food. "When did you come in? I didn't hear you."

Hannah looked off into the distance, not sure if her mom was asking when she got back to the house, or when she came into the kitchen. She was thankful that her going out into the woods wasn't just her imagination.

"Oh, I was just up in my room and I decided to come down." Hannah said, stepping forward, hoping that her mom would say something that could explain how Hannah had gotten from the forest beyond the cemetery back to her room.

"That's nice, honey. Did you have a nice time

exploring outside?"

"Yeah, I did. I found this willow tree and it's beautiful. I laid down on the stone bench underneath it and I felt so relaxed." Hannah looked away and sighed. "It was peaceful."

"That's good, you've been needing some of that. Peace and quiet is what we all need nowadays after living in New York for three years."

Hannah smiled and looked back at her mom. For some reason, thinking back on New York memories made Hannah feel small, like a tiny mouse running through an endless maze of angry pedestrians and rude cab drivers.

"I hope you're hungry because this chicken casserole looks amazing." Martha interrupted Hannah's shrinking feeling.

Hannah looked at her mother, the memories of New York fading into her subconscious. She'd had some good times in New York, but it was mostly sad and terrible memories now…

Hannah was happy to let New York City fade into the distance of time.

"Could you shred some cheese, honey?" Martha asked.

"Sure." Hannah passed between her mom and the

island, seeing what she was making in the pot. Yum, it was her favorite soup—tomato.

Hannah grabbed the cheese out of the fridge, then picked up the bowl and grater off the island and set the bowl down on the counter between the refrigerator and the sink. She positioned the grater over the bowl and raised the cheese.

"And remember to be careful, it could slice your skin right off!"

Hannah flinched at her mother's tone. She understood the dangers, but she had asked Hannah to do it. But she knew if she complained that her mom had told her this a hundred times before, Martha would merely remind her that she was Hannah's mom—and she had every reason to remind her.

Hannah rolled her eyes at the memories. "I know, Mom. You know I'll be careful."

And before her mom could say another word on the subject she began shredding the cheese.

"You know those kids we met earlier were really nice. Who knows... you could end up being best friends with them."

Hannah could tell this was one of her mom's form of

small talk. Those small talks usually held a long subject, but could be brought up whenever it happened to pop into her head.

Hannah was grateful to know that she hadn't imagined meeting them. They had been nice.

"That boy was kinda cute. Who knows... maybe in the future..."

"Mom! Don't!" Hannah stopped her mom before she could go on with that train of thought.

The last boy that Martha had liked for Hannah, she had suggested that Hannah ask him out. He had turned out to be more interested in Martha than Hannah, which still made her want to barf.

"I was just saying that you might go out with him sometime in the future." Martha said, innocently shrugging her shoulders.

"Eww." Hannah said, shrugging the conversation off and shaking her head vigorously, hoping that would be enough to get her mother to stop pushing.

"I can't even think about dating right now." Which was true. Hannah had a whole long list in her head about stuff more important than dating.

"Okay, I was just voicing some of my opinions."

Martha defended.

Hannah quietly sighed and rolled her eyes.

She was almost done grating the cheese when she felt her right index finger slide across one of the blades. A sound barely escaped from Hannah's mouth as she jumped back from the counter. She had cut herself only a few times, but after the first two she learned how to hide it from her mom so she wouldn't worry.

But when Hannah looked down at her finger, she was shocked to see that there wasn't even a scratch. No blood. Only a light pinkish color that made her skin look like she had been pressing on it hard.

Hannah was confused and a little frightened, staring at her finger as if it were a foreign object and not her own finger. The grater should have cut her finger.

Shouldn't it?

Hannah was so filled with confusion and concern and fear, her hand started to shake—but when her thoughts started to race, she stopped it. Stopped the shaking. Stopped the racing. And did her best to wipe any look of concern or nerves off her face.

She pushed every nervous thought to the very back of her mind. Her body wanted to rebel and tremble, but

Hannah refused to succumb and show her mother how afraid she was.

Hannah knew she couldn't tell her mother about the weird things that were happening to her. Hannah had no doubt that her mother would believe her, but she has had too much to deal with as it was. Divorce. Losing her father. Moving her kids to a different state... again.

Hannah had convinced herself it would be better to not say anything to her mom, but she had to make herself stop staring at her finger. Then she squared her shoulders, picked up the tool again, and finished grating the cheese. Then she rinsed the cheese grater off and picked up the bowl of cheese—and had turned to carry it over to the table, when her mother's voice stopped her.

"Where did you get that necklace?"

Hannah's face scrunched up, trying to figure out just what her mom was talking about. She turned to face her mom and followed her mother's eyes focusing on her shirt. There she saw a silver necklace in the shape of a crescent moon filled with more silver pieces that were woven into crisscrossing knots, on a leather chain around her neck.

Surprise filled her. She had never seen this necklace before in her life. She'd never even noticed the thing around her neck until her mother had mentioned it.

Hannah lifted it up with her right hand. It was light. It was obviously made of some sort of metal, but it was so light.

Weird.

Even though she had just noticed it, she felt an odd connection to the necklace—which freaked her out a little. She dropped it, letting it hang around her neck.

"It was just hanging around." Which was the truth, it was just hanging around Hannah's neck. Even though Hannah hadn't a clue to its origin.

"Well it's pretty." Martha smiled at her daughter.

"Thanks." Hannah said, smiling back, thinking this was yet another strange thing to add to the list of strange things that had happened to her recently.

Hannah turned and left the kitchen as quickly as possible and walked to the right, opposite to where she'd come from. She stopped and leaned her back against the wall.

She glanced over to the door across from her. Right in front of her, Zoe and Ryan were sitting at the dining table —chatting.

On the inside, she felt like panicking. She'd gone to the cemetery and fallen asleep on an oddly comfy stone bench. She'd then woken up in her room, with no idea of how she'd gotten there. Now she had this necklace around her neck — one that she'd never seen before.

And... it seemed like she couldn't be cut or scratched easily. Anymore.

What is going on?

Seeing her siblings gave her a sense of normalcy. The thought of protecting them calmed her down. She was also grateful she'd been able to avoid lying to her mom.

Martha didn't much like it when Hannah and Zoe were doing things that involved strange or spooky things —like surfing the internet trying to figure out what had caused Zoe's accident. Martha had made them quit searching and told them that everything would be fine, that Zoe was safe and that the police would handle it. But that hadn't prevented Zoe from having nightmares until she was nine years old.

Thinking of how close she had come to losing Zoe, Hannah felt the need to be close to her, close to them both.

She pushed herself away from the wall and walked toward the dining room.

A FAMILY DINNER

Hannah sat down at the dinner table. Zoe and Ryan already sat across from each other.

She wanted to ask one of them if they had been near the cemetery... they might have seen something. But she decided to wait until her mom came in.

She sat down next to Zoe, watching her siblings talk, debating about a movie that had been released at the end of June.

Ryan was complaining that a kid in the movie had been screaming way too much, while Zoe made the point that she was under a lot of stress. Her home was being attacked and she had the right to freak out since she was only a kid.

Hannah felt warmed at the sight of her siblings. Their conversation faded into the background a little, but she still watched them. She felt like she had missed so much time with them when they were in New York. Ryan had his friends that he would have play dates with… and by play dates, she meant he and his buddies would get together and play the most violent video games they could get their hands on.

But Zoe only had her books. She would wake up in the morning, eat breakfast, read a book while on the ride to school, read more at lunch while sitting by herself, read more on the way home and continue reading until dinner. Once dinner was over she would read until she went to sleep.

Hannah refused to be the type of person that graduates high school, goes to college and never sees her siblings, except for holidays. She might have to wait until Ryan was out of his cootie stage in life, but when he was older she could try to mend their relationship. But Zoe, she could fix that now... after all, they did partner up after Zoe's accident. Hannah did save her and she wasn't gonna let that go to waste now.

Zoe looked over at Hannah and said something. Hannah shook her thoughts away and focused on her sister's face.

"What?"

"Are you all right?" Zoe asked, her tone filled with humor and concern—a tone that Hannah was not unfamiliar with nowadays.

"I'm fine. Never better." Hannah couldn't believe the smile that she felt spreading across her face and it was real. Her answer was real.

She'd expected a lie to roll off her tongue, but it was all true. Moving to Shadowhill, wishing to be closer to her siblings, leaving New York in the past. It all made her feel better. Except for that nagging feeling in her stomach that something weird was happening—something that meant that her life had changed forever.

It felt like her mom took forever to finish up dinner and come to the table. But eventually she showed up.

Hannah was partly relieved, but the worries of all the weird, recent events bubbled up from her stomach. Martha had carried in a large bowl of tomato soup and the dish containing the chicken casserole. She set it on the table, then she went around her daughters to sit next to Ryan and across from Hannah. Zoe and Ryan quickly started filling their plates.

"So guys, how has your day been?" Martha asked as she began scooping chicken casserole onto her plate.

"I really like my room, but the house itself is a little hideous." Ryan said.

Hannah could almost hear the roll of Zoe's eyes, but her body language was completely positive.

"I think it's a good change of scenery!" Zoe chimed in, not admitting to the eye roll. Hannah almost smiled at her sister's spunk.

"And you, Hannah?" Martha asked. "Do you like it here?"

Hannah looked down at her empty plate as Zoe started scooping chicken casserole onto her plate. "I do, so far."

Now was her chance to ask her question—the one that had been eating her alive since her mother walked in the room. Though she'd just come in and sat down, the seconds had felt like hours.

"Have any of you been in the cemetery?" Hannah asked, trying to sound non-accusative, but just naturally curious.

Zoe stopped filling her plate, with her hand holding the scoop of food in mid air. She glanced around the table without looking up; she could tell that there was something strange about Hannah's mannerism.

"No, I don't think that I'll ever step foot in there!" Ryan said almost immediately and he stuffed his mouth full of the casserole.

"I haven't yet, but I hope to be able to explore it soon. You never know what mysterious things you might find in there." Zoe said.

This made Hannah curious. She stared at her sister while Zoe sat eating her share of the casserole. After figuring out that she wasn't going to divulge anymore information, Hannah looked away while their mom and Ryan continued to stare at Zoe.

"What? We all like different things." Zoe defended.

Hannah looked to her mom now, hoping and praying that she would have an answer that would help her worries, since she was practically on the edge of her seat.

"I haven't been there, either." Martha said with a shrug, Hannah slumped back in her chair, trying to seem nonchalant,. She may have failed in her acting skills because Zoe stared at her for a few moments before she went back to eating her food.

And that was it.

No one seemed to know how she had gotten back to her room. No one else knew which room was her's. Hannah had thought about sleepwalking, but she had never sleep-walked in her entire life.

"Did you enjoy exploring, Hannah?" Martha asked.

"Yeah. I did." Hannah said, trying not to sound disappointed.

She knew she hadn't dreamed the weird event. Her mom remembered meeting Kiki and Jack and her mom knew that she'd went to explore outside. Not to mention noticing the necklace…

Where did it come from?

And who had brought her back... because if no one had, how had she gotten back to her room?

"Aren't you hungry?" Martha asked her, motioning toward Hannah's empty plate. Hannah realized that she hadn't eaten yet and her mom had went to the trouble of making her favorite soup.

"Yeah. I am." She sat up straight and started filling her

plate. She did her best to get through dinner with a straight face, but it wasn't easy at all.

After dinner, Martha gave Hannah her lamp so she could read in her room before she fell asleep—something she didn't do often but when she did it, Martha was the only person Hannah told about it.

Hannah escaped to her room. Her mind was full of thoughts she couldn't seem to straighten out. So she grabbed her earbuds and her cell phone and picked her favorite calming noises to listen to while she read.

She lay on her bed and listened to waves crashing and a fire crackling, with Pumpkin at her side. After awhile, she almost fell asleep—and the many conversations she'd had with her mother about the dangers of sleeping with wired headphones popped into her head. So she turned off the calming noises and removed her headphones.

"Hannah!" She heard her mother call out.

"Hannah!" At the second call, Hannah left her room and followed her mom's voice and found her not too far from her room.

"What is it, mom?" Hannah asked when she saw her.

"I just wanted to say goodnight, sweetie. And I didn't know which room you picked." Martha said.

"I'm in the last room down that hall." Hannah said, pointing behind her.

"Good to know. Goodnight, honey."

"Goodnight, mom." Hannah and her mom hugged for another second or two—and then parted ways, heading down their separate halls.

Hannah walked to her room in silence. Once there, she changed into her soft, warm, moon and star themed pajamas. From a large bag she pulled out her pillow and her favorite soft, vampire themed blanket.

After placing both things on her mattress, Hannah laid down on the bed, but noticed a small, cold feeling on her neck—which made her realize that she hadn't taken off the mystery necklace. She got out of bed and Pumpkin took the opportunity to steal the warm spot on the bed away from Hannah.

She approached her smaller bag and opened one of the side pockets—and then stared as she left the necklace hanging from her fingers. She couldn't seem to let it go, to be apart from it for eight hours. She shook away the longing to hang it around her neck and then tucked it away safely in her smaller bag.

The she sighed and turned away from her necklace and returned to her mattress, pushing Pumpkin out of the way just enough so she could actually have room on the bed. Then she turned off her lamp and tried to block out the thoughts of the necklace, the willow tree, the cheese grater and then, even though the pit in her stomach continued to grow and churn, she somehow managed to drift off to sleep.

A WHISPER IN THE NIGHT

September 15th, 2018. 2:35 a.m.

The wind blew through the silence of the night. Bats danced in the air. Nocturnal creatures crept on the ground. A gentle voice warmed the air, waking Hannah with a gentle breeze.

Hannah moaned and turned in her bed, wiping her cheek where the wind blew.

"Hannah." The voice was louder now, more insistent.

Hannah's eyes shot open.

"Hannah."

Hannah sat up. The voice was female, familiar, almost motherly.

"Hannah."

Hannah pushed aside her blanket, stood up and looked around her room. No one was in the room with her.

It was odd, she could see every nook and cranny in her dark room. The only light in the room was the moon — and it didn't seem terribly bright, but she could see as clearly as if it were the sun lighting up her room. She rubbed at her eyes and then looked again.

Could I be dreaming again?

Maybe, but she didn't feel like she had in the other dream. Now she felt wide awake.

"Guess this is what comes next." Hannah said aloud, to anyone who might be listening.

But no one else was there.

She wanted to curl back up on her mattress and go back to sleep, but as soon as she thought about it, the voice rang out again.

"Hannah." The voice sung.

Clearly, Hannah was supposed to investigate this faceless voice.

"Hannah."

Her bedroom door creaked open. As she watched, the wind blew through the door.

"Hannah."

She sighed and resigned herself to walking out into the hall.

She looked out into the dark hall. Again, not a single light could be seen from the other rooms. She shook her head. She'd never had especially good vision in the dark before. But now, she could see every door, every little detail in the carpet, even into the edges where the ceiling joined the walls.

This is more than a little eerie.

She wanted to stop, to turn around and go back into her room, go back to sleep, but somehow she knew that the voice would not stop, so she started down the hall. She looked down to the opening under Zoe's door as she passed it. She almost wanted to wake her sister up, to beg her to come with her. Zoe knew about weird stuff. This was much more Zoe's forte, than it was Hannah's.

But in spite of how much she wanted to wake her sister, she didn't. She hadn't actually told her about the list of strange things that had been happening lately, so Zoe wouldn't understand why Hannah had woken her up in the middle of the night. Better to just go on and get this over with... without waking anyone else up. So, she kept going past her sister's door and continued following the voice to the grand stairs.

"Hannah." The voice sounded almost taunting this time.

Hannah followed the voice to the right side of the house, heading for unknown territory for her. She'd explored outside, but it was so late after they'd finished dinner—and she hadn't taken any time to look through the house.

"Hannah." The voice whispered, but somehow it seemed to be growing louder... closer.

She feared any moment a stranger... or a monster like from that dream... was gonna jump out in front of her and tackle her.

"Hannah."

Still, she followed the voice. To the end of the hall, where she turned to the right. Then she shuddered at the sound of a different voice... sounding unexpectedly from right behind her.

"Hannah?"

She turned back quickly, expecting something awful, but it was Ryan.

"Hannah." The first voice called. It sounded sort of singsong like now. It urged her to follow, but she couldn't, now that Ryan was here.

"What are you doing?" Ryan asked.

"Nothing." Hannah answered. "What are you doing here? You shouldn't be up at this hour." Hannah added.

"I was in the kitchen getting a snack." Ryan answered. He sounded grumpy. Something must have woken him up too. Or else he'd gotten to that stage of tired where he was fighting going to sleep... like he had when he was much younger. It always made him grumpy.

Yeah, yeah. Well, come on, I'll walk you back." Hannah held him by the shoulders and steered him in the direction of his room, until he shrugged her off and walked a little faster to get ahead of her.

They walked up the stairs and then down the hall, and

Ryan went to the third door on the right.

"Good night Ryan." Hannah said after she had gently pushed him toward his room.

"Yeah, yeah, good night." Ryan said as he closed the door behind him.

"I knew it. They're all crazy."

Hannah heard her brother's voice through the door. She rolled her eyes at his comment. He'd pretty much always thought that Hannah and Zoe were crazy. It was probably just a little brother thing—to think your older sisters are crazy.

Hannah debated then... about going back to where the mystery voice had been leading her. But it had stopped now and it was still either very late in the night... or else very early in the morning. So, Hannah headed back to her room, grateful not to hear the mysterious voice trying to persuade her away.

When she got back to her room, Pumpkin lifted her head from her resting spot on the bed. She must not have moved since Hannah left, because Hannah still had her own space in the bed. The small black bag on the floor caught Hannah's attention for some reason. She reached down, opened the side pocket and pulled out the necklace. When she draped it around her neck, Pumpkin whimpered.

"I know, I know." Hannah said as she crawled back into bed.

Pumpkin laid her head down on Hannah's chest and fell asleep, while Hannah sleepily rubbed the top of her dog's head. She listened for the voice for a few minutes but finally gave up and closed her eyes, finally drifting off to sleep.

"Hannah." The voice whispered. "Oh Hannah. I'm coming to you, Hannah." That same mysterious voice sung in its taunting tone.

Hannah left her room and made her way to the stairs.

"Come to me, Hannah." The voice sang as Hannah walked down the stairs.

All the windows were open and the white curtains flowed in the moonlight like water. The cold air sent shivers over Hannah's skin. She turned and walked down the last long hall. She didn't feel fear anymore. She felt nothing but a single-minded need, like her only thought and goal in life was to follow this voice and find out why it was calling her. She made her way to a door that was near where Ryan had stopped her before.

"Hannah. Almost there, Hannah." The voice whispered as Hannah faced the door and all the fear flooded back into her bones. The voice had changed a little, it was deeper, almost male.

"Just turn the knob, Hannah." The voice whispered, and yet it sounded louder again—as if the person that was calling her was right next to her.

"Help me!" An obviously female voice called.

"It's easy. You know what to do." The almost male voice called.

Hannah wanted to turn and run back to her room, but instead she was reaching for the knob. She felt like she had no control over her body, like she was stuck in her mind and couldn't control anything but her mouth and eyes. She was doing the exact opposite of what she wanted to do.

"No!" Hannah screamed. She tried to be quiet so she wouldn't wake her family.

"Come Hannah, help us, or we can't go." The voice said and Hannah screamed louder than before, this time not caring about waking her family. She wanted them awake to come find her.

Hannah opened the door and out jumped the monster that she'd seen in her dream. Fangs, claws and the same pale skin. The monster leaped on her and snarled at her.

As Hannah struggled with the monster, she saw dark clouds form on the ceiling and another voice yelled.

"Wake up!" this one was familiar, it sounded like Zoe but it sounded almost ghostly.

The monster held Hannah down as it began to lean down. Its fangs started to get close to her neck.

"No!" Hannah yelled! She screamed and thrashed, anything to stop this beast from biting her and most likely giving her some sort of disease.

And then Hannah's eyes opened as she sat up in her bed. Zoe was sitting right next to her on the bed.

"What, where?" Hannah started.

"You're in your room, sis." Zoe said.

"Why are...?" Hannah started again, but Zoe interrupted her.

"I heard you yelling in your sleep, I figured that you were having a bad dream so I came to wake you up."

"Thanks, sis." Hannah said. She didn't say anything else though. She wanted to express her gratitude, but was afraid if she said too much, she would end up telling Zoe all about the dream—and the other dream from before and then everything would end up spilling out.

"Wanna talk about it?" Zoe asked.

Hannah thought about it. It might be nice to finally tell her sister about all of the weird things that were happening to her, but she didn't want to burden her with something she didn't really ask for.

But on the other hand she had just asked if Hannah wanted to talk about it, so Hannah decided then and there. "Sure."

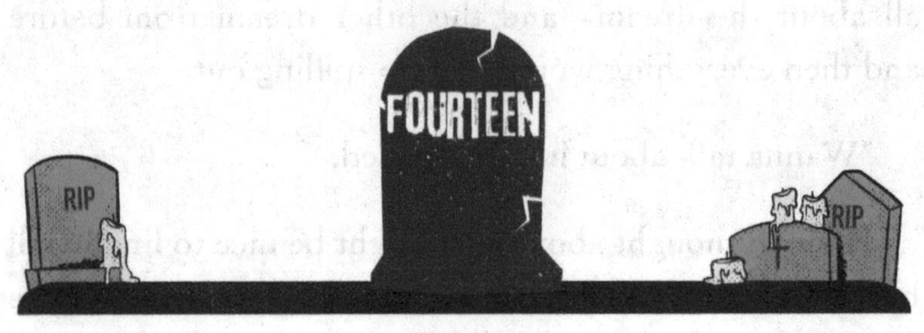

CONFIDANT

Hannah took a deep breath, suddenly nervous about telling the entire story to her little sister. Zoe waited, looking expectantly—and Hannah knew she should just get it over with.

So, she launched into the story of the dream... her nightmare first. Somehow, she knew that she hadn't dreamed the first time hearing the voice, because the moon hung around her neck.

She told the entire story, not leaving anything out, but

maybe glossing over a few of the more terrifying parts.

She sighed as she finished the story of her nightmare. Then she looked at her sister, her blue eyes looking down at Hannah curiously. All that was left to do was to tell Zoe the rest of it. Soon there would be no secrets between them.

Hannah looked down and took a deep breath, then looked up as she released it.

"Zoe?" Hannah's voice was shaky. She wanted to turn back, to not risk ruining the possibility of a future relationship with her sister.

"Yes?" Zoe's voice reflected her curiosity, her head tilted slightly.

Hannah knew she could still turn back, still not go all the way to explaining what a freak she felt like... hearing voices, doors breaking, falling asleep and not remembering how she got somewhere else. But she really didn't want to stop. Her heart was telling her to finish.

"We're sisters. And while that doesn't exactly cement anything between us, we should be able to trust each other with secrets... Right?" Hannah's shoulders had turned in and her chin had lowered, as if she were trying to hide herself.

"Of course." Zoe agreed with Hannah.

"But what if there's a secret between us that could change our lives forever. And you may never think of me the same way again." Tears began to pool in her eyes. She wiped at her cheeks and tried to stop the tears from falling.

Zoe cupped Hannah's face with her hands, making Hannah look into her eyes. "There is nothing that you could tell me that would make me *not* love you." Zoe lowered her hands to rest in her lap and stared at her sister.

Hannah smiled a little.

"Tell me." Zoe insisted in a tone that Hannah couldn't deny.

So, she explained in as much detail as she could remember. She explained about her strength, about being able to see in the dark, about not getting cut by the cheese grater, going into the woods, falling asleep and waking up on her bed. And finally she explained the necklace and how she didn't know it's origin.

"Yep. If I didn't know any better I'd say that you're dreaming about vampires." Zoe said.

"But I don't understand why this is happening to me."

"Sometimes we don't have the answers right away, we just have to deal with it till we figure it out." Zoe said, smiling.

"So you're not freaked?" Hannah looked down, regretting her question as she said it.

"No."

Hannah looked up at her sister.

"Honestly, it kinda makes me respect you a bit more…"

Hannah tilted her head curiously.

"I always thought that all you thought about in life was nail polish, parties, guys and stuff that really wasn't all that important… but now that I see that you don't, and it makes me more proud of you." Zoe said.

Grateful tears flooded Hannah's eyes and she gathered Zoe up in a hug. She was careful not to squeeze too tightly, especially since Zoe was all too aware of her freaky strength now.

"Come on, get dressed, let's go downstairs, and eat breakfast." Zoe ordered as she stood up.

"You're always looking after me." Hannah said as she got out of bed and stood up. "Even when I'm the one who should be looking after you, cuz you've been through so much crap."

"Well I suppose, just cuz some weird thing in Lake Rikersfield tried to drown me." Zoe said.

"And someone kidnapped you, don't forget that!" Hannah corrected.

"How could I?" Zoe said, heading for the door and opening it.

"You don't still have nightmares do you?" Hannah asked.

"No don't be silly, if I was it would be because of that creature in Lake Rikersfield." Zoe said smiling nervously then shuddered quietly. "Now get dressed or Ryan'll eat your breakfast." And she motioned for Hannah to get dressed.

Hannah looked at what Zoe was wearing, black tennis shoes, jeans, a red short-sleeve shirt, and her brown hair, tied in a ponytail.

"I'm gonna go protect our food." Zoe said and she left the room. "See you down there!"

Hannah looked through her smaller bag for clothes. She picked out a dark teal short-sleeve shirt, jeans, and her black tennis shoes. After getting dressed, Hannah ran her brush through her hair then went downstairs to save her breakfast.

"Hey guys!" Hannah said as she came into the dinning room. She sat next to Zoe, who had her hands protectively covering two plates of eggs and pancakes, while watching Ryan—who was looking awful mischievously at Zoe... and the plates in front of her and Hannah.

Zoe placed one of the plates in front of Hannah, still watching Ryan. "You know Hannah, after the movers come and set up your room you could call that boy Jack and see if he wanted to show you the town." Martha suggested.

"Mom, why must you push me?" Hannah groaned, completely *not* in the mood to be thinking about boys.

"Who is this and why haven't I heard about him?" Zoe asked, her tone had somehow gone from sweet little sister to protective big sister.

"Just someone who came to welcome us to the neighborhood and his friend who wanted to see the house." Hannah answered, before her mother could give her siblings the wrong idea.

"I just want you to have a friend, sweetie." Martha said.

"I have one." Hannah gestured to her sister, "Zoe."

"Yeah." To Hannah's surprise, Zoe agreed really quickly—and sounded pretty absolute in her answer.

It was nice to know. She'd been afraid that, after all these years of a not so good relationship, Zoe would hold a grudge. But her little sister was definitely more surprising than Hannah had thought. With a smile, she started digging into her food.

"Someone besides your sister. No offense, Zoe." Martha said.

"Offense taken." Zoe joked.

"Zoe...!" Martha started, but stopped when Hannah interrupted.

"Fine, I'll give Kiki a call!" Hannah said.

"You don't even have to wait for the movers. You could go right after breakfast." Martha said.

"Okay." Hannah said, rolling her eyes. "By the way, where is the cinnamon and sugar?"

"Mom forgot it again." Zoe said as she played with her eggs with a sad, annoyed look on her face.

"Who's side are you on?" Martha asked Zoe.

"My own." Zoe said in a surprising regal tone.

Hannah ran to the kitchen for the cinnamon and sugar.

Hannah stopped in the door and felt the hairs on the back of her neck stand up—and realized that she felt as if she was being watched. She looked around the kitchen.

Nothing. No one else was there.

She grabbed the cinnamon and sugar off the island and headed back to the dining room.

After breakfast, the two sisters ended up back in Hannah's room, where Hannah told Zoe about feeling like she was being watched.

"Strange." Zoe said.

"I know." Hannah agreed.

"Hannah." Zoe tried to interrupt, but Hannah continued.

"Who would be watching me? Who knows we're even here?"

"Hannah!" Zoe said, her voice sounding more than a little panicked.

"What?" Hannah asked.

Zoe pointed outside, not taking her eyes off the thing she was looking at.

Hannah turned, followed the direction of her sister's pointing finger and saw a person dressed in all black, standing in the cemetery, watching the house.

Answers... was the single thought that crossed Hannah's mind, but she pushed that thought to the back of her mind. She was not going to endanger herself or her family by chasing after a crazy person who was watching their house.

Fear crept into her body, holding her firmly to her spot in the room.

Without really even knowing what she was doing, Hannah slipped the necklace under her shirt and pulled her eyes away from the stranger and back to her sister, who was gone.

Hannah could hear her running down the hall. She took off running after her.

At first it was hard for Hannah to keep up with her, but she found every step was easier and easier. By the time they were actually getting close to the cemetery, the man was gone.

Zoe stopped so suddenly, Hannah ran into her and they both went crashing to the ground. As they fell, Hannah managed to pull Zoe toward her and shift her weight so Zoe fell on top of Hannah and not the ground.

Zoe rolled off of Hannah and looked back toward the cemetery, first making sure nothing was going to attack them—and then second, to see if she could see where whoever was watching them had gone.

Hannah pushed herself into a sitting position—and then just sat there on the ground with her legs tucked to the side. She looked over at her sister and sighed.

"Why did you run toward danger? To the person we don't know, who could have kidnapped us or killed us." Hannah asked, her breath coming out in little puffs of frustration.

"I don't know why, but I thought he might have answers." Zoe said as if she worried she was being ridiculous.

Hannah waited a minute before she agreed. "I did, too."

"Why don't we just call Kiki and see if her offer still stands, and try to get this off your mind." Zoe said, standing up.

"Okay." Hannah said as Zoe helped her up.

Hannah took a few deep breaths, then got out her phone, but before she could dial the number Zoe stopped her.

"Everything'll be okay, sis." Zoe said.

If Zoe could be convinced, certainly Hannah could. "I know." Hannah said, trying to believe her sister, but failing to completely believe herself.

Hannah went back to the phone and dialed Kiki's number. The other line rang only once.

"Hello." Kiki answered on her end of the line.

"Hello, it's Hannah from yesterday... the one who moved into the haunted house?" Hannah said, hoping she wasn't that forgettable.

"Oh yeah, I remember you, I have a very good memory." Kiki said.

"Who are you on the phone with, young lady!" A voice on Kiki's end hollered.

"No one, Grandmother!" Kiki answered the voice.

"See you don't even know who your daughter talks to on that death machine!" Kiki's grandmother yelled, then came the noise of glass shattering.

"I was just wondering if I could take you up on your offer, about showing me the town." Hannah asked. She was definitely curious about what was going on at Kiki's house, but that was best left until they could ask her in person. It sounded like it would be a good story—and would be an excellent distraction.

"Sure, I'll be there in five minutes." Kiki said. "Is it okay if I bring Jack?"

"Sure, I'm bringing my sister." Hannah said.

"Ooh, I'd love to meet her." Kiki bubbled.

"Okay see y..." But there was already silence on the line. Kiki must have hung up in her haste to get back to the "haunted" house.

EXPLORING SHADOWHILL

Hannah didn't bother going in the house, but Zoe took the opportunity to run in and grab a sweater. Just as five minutes passed, Zoe came back—and Kiki and Jack appeared at the end of the driveway.

"Sure you don't want your sweater?" Zoe asked as Hannah stood.

"I'm sure." Hannah answered—and they started walking toward their new friends.

When they reached Kiki and Jack, they noticed another person with them. A girl about Kiki and Hannah's age. Kiki had her hair in a braid, and wore jeans, the same blue flip flops, and a yellow long-sleeve turtleneck sweater. Jack wore a light gray short-sleeve shirt, jeans, and brown tennis shoes.

The mystery girl had light brown hair, soft eyes that were a dark teal color. She wore a long denim skirt, tan tennis shoes and a tan long-sleeve shirt with silver etchings of native American symbols. She looked shy and timid.

She kind of reminded Hannah of Zoe whenever Maggie had dragged them both to a party.

"Zoe, this is Kiki and Jack." Hannah introduced them all. "And guys this is Zoe."

They both greeted Zoe with smiles. "Hannah, Zoe. This is my sister Mera." Kiki said, motioning to the mystery girl. "I brought her with me so that she could get away from our grandmother who's visiting this week." Kiki explained.

"Oh, it's nice to meet you, Mera." Hannah said.

The only response she got was a shy, half smile.

Zoe walked between Kiki and Jack, right up to Mera.

"Hi, it's nice to meet you." She held out her hand to Mera, who looked at first like she wasn't going to take it, but after a few seconds she took Zoe's hand and smiled. "Nice to meet you."

Mera's voice was quiet. Hannah thought that must mean she was Kiki's younger sister. Shyness seemed to be a younger sibling trait.

Well... not all younger siblings.

She was thinking of Ryan, of course. He was anything but shy.

"Well, shall we get going?" Kiki asked. Everyone nodded and started down the driveway.

Once they reached the end of the long driveway, Jack led the group away from their house and toward town, with Zoe and Mera right beside him.

Kiki and Hannah were a few steps behind them. They came to Main Street first. It was busier than Hannah had expected of such a small town. The street was filled with people and cars going in all different directions... kinda like they had in New York.

They went to the small video store on Main Street, a clothing shop—where Jack stayed outside to wait for them. Then, at the other end of Main Street, they went down High Noon Ridge until they got to the library, which Zoe enjoyed immensely. It was all they could do to drag her away.

By that time it was lunchtime and Kiki led them back to Main Street and into a restaurant.

"It's on us, so get whatever you want." Kiki said, then shot Jack a look, who looked as if he hadn't been expecting to help pay for lunch. Hannah picked up the menu—which Jack, Mera and Kiki didn't seem to need to look at.

When the harried waitress came over, Hannah waved to Jack. He ordered first. He got a cheeseburger with only mustard on it. Kiki went next, she got a bacon, lettuce, and tomato sandwich. Zoe got a chicken sandwich with mayo and lettuce. Mera got a chicken sandwich with tomato. Hannah went last, she got a cheeseburger with ketchup, mustard, lettuce, and tomato on it.

During their short lunch, they talked about a lot of things... Shadowhill, New York, why the Autumns had moved there from such a big city. Zoe and Hannah began to forget about all the worries that were left at the new house.

They also forgot about the necklace that was hanging around Hannah's neck, the willow tree and the dreams that were plaguing Hannah.

After lunch Kiki, Mera and Jack took Hannah and Zoe to a bookstore—again, a place that was difficult to drag Zoe away from. They stopped in at a beauty salon that looked like it was right out of an old television show. Then they went to a magic store.

When they walked in, all sorts of different smells filled the air. There was cinnamon, pumpkin, sage and some other spices hanging in the air, along with the smell of books—which Zoe recognized right away and commented on. And as a finishing touch, there was a woodsy smell that hung over all the other scents. The store was small—not small like you could only fit five or six people in it, more like fifteen or twenty—but definitely a cozy space.

"Hey Mr. Morrison." Kiki called to the man behind the counter.

"Hello Kiki, Jack, Mera." Mr. Morrison said. His voice held affection for each name, but even more for Mera. It made Hannah think he must know her the best. "And who are these new people?"

"This is Hannah and her sister Zoe." Kiki said as she motioned toward her new friends.

"Hi, you may find me in here more often than you

think." Zoe smiled as she waved to Mr. Morrison.

Beside the counter were several small steps leading down and farther into the store, Zoe wasted no time taking off down into that area to look at the books that filled a few shelves. Kiki was looking at small knick knacks to the right of the store, close to the door... not in the area where Zoe was. Mera continued to talk quietly, while Jack remained standing close to Hannah.

"Is there anything specific I can help you find?" Mr. Morrison asked.

"No, we're just looking." Hannah replied.

"So, what do you think of Shadowhill so far?" Jack asked.

"I think I like it so far. It's just the change my mom needs."

"What about you?" Jack asked, Hannah turned to him, her eyebrows tilted up in a clear question. "What do you need?"

Hannah shrugged.

"I don't know anymore." Hannah shrugged, then walked over to Kiki with Jack following. She looked at small crystals of different colors, white, green, lime green, light and dark blue, purple, yellow, orange, red, and black.

Hannah picked up a green one that intrigued her for some reason — and looked for a price tag.

She saw one that said "Crystals $3.49" but that price seemed ridiculously cheap when she compared it to some of the prices they'd paid in New York. She held onto the crystal she'd picked up.

Then thinking of Zoe, Hannah picked up an orange one. "I'm gonna go ask Zoe about something." Hannah said to Kiki and Jack.

"Okay." Kiki said in return.

Hannah was already walking away toward Zoe. She was not a bit surprised to find her sister still looking at the books. "Hey, look at what I found." Hannah said as she opened her hand to show Zoe.

Zoe pulled herself away from the books and looked into Hannah's hand.

"Oh my goodness, crystals." Zoe said. "Both of our favorite colors, too."

"I was thinking that we could make necklaces out of them." Hannah said.

"Sure, works for me." Zoe shrugged. "Look at what I

found." Zoe said as she held up a book, it had a leather cover, with the word "Legends" on it.

"Wow, that's nice." Hannah agreed.

"Yeah, it is." Zoe said as she took the orange crystal out of Hannah's hand, Hannah was a bit puzzled, but didn't question her sister.

"You pay for your stuff. I'll pay for mine." Zoe said.

"Okay." Hannah said, a bit confused at why Zoe would insist on buying something she had not specifically picked up herself.

Honestly, there was no predicting how her sister's mind would work. So she let it go and turned back toward Kiki and Jack with a smile. She had been making an effort to smile more recently. It still felt a little foreign to her, but it was a welcome change. Zoe shared her smile —even though they shared little else in the looks department.

Hannah joined Zoe in book browsing for a few minutes until Kiki, Jack and Mera joined them.

"Hey, did you find anything?" Kiki asked.

"Just books and crystals." Zoe answered.

"You will not be disappointed with the books. Mr.

Morrison has good books, not boring at all."

"I agree, usually I don't read, but Kiki forced me to read one that she got from this store and I didn't want to put it down. My mom wondered if I was an imposter." Jack told her.

He, Hannah and Kiki laughed. Mera and Zoe just smiled.

"Did you guys find anything?" Hannah asked, Jack shook his head.

"I found a heart shaped crystal." Kiki said happily as she opened her hand to show it off.

"I didn't see those." Hannah said.

"I can show you where they are." Kiki said, motioning to the place where Hannah had found the crystals.

"No, it's fine. I like this one." She told Kiki, before her new friend could pull her over to the crystals.

"Okay. Are you guys ready to go, then?" Kiki asked.

They all agreed and Zoe, Hannah, Kiki, Mera and Jack all walked to the counter.

Kiki went first. Jack didn't get anything so once she paid, Zoe went next, then Hannah.

PLAY DUMB

They completed the tour by 5:30 p.m. at the end of High Noon Ridge where it connected with Sunset Road.

"We have to get home." Kiki said.

"Your mom and grandma fighting again?" Jack asked.

"Yes, and I can't be on the phone any more, because grandmother cut all the phone cords, not to mention the TV. She cut the cord then shot it, right in the middle of the screen too. Dad was not happy about that at all. He almost started to scream at her, but mom got between them." Kiki said.

"Where were you two?" Jack asked.

"Mostly outside, I went inside to get my phone when Hannah called. Then I went back outside, but that didn't help, when I was about to hang up, grandmother came out and took my phone, then she threw it on the ground and stomped on it." Kiki explained.

"That's why you got cut off mid-sentence." Hannah said.

Kiki nodded.

"Somehow, someway, we've survived not sending her to a home, but ever since she's gotten hold of a gun, life has gotten a bit more interesting." Mera concluded.

"How did she get hold of a gun?" Zoe asked.

Zoe expected Mera to shy away from the question, but she didn't. "We don't know. Kiki and I woke up one morning and she was shooting at the neighbors outdoor TV."

"Luckily our dad got to her before she destroyed the TV. But the neighbors weren't happy about the whole thing. And whenever dad takes away her gun, she gets it back or maybe she just gets a different one somehow.

And we have no clue how or when she's doing all of this."

No sooner had Kiki finished her sentence than an elderly lady started down the sidewalk of Sunset Road, yelling and shaking her cane in the air. A man and a woman about Hannah's parent's ages were following her… arguing with her.

"Your family?" Hannah asked, gesturing toward them.

"Is it that obvious?" Kiki asked. She said it in a way that told them she already knew the answer. She and Mera both looked like they wanted to shrink away and hide from their family.

"Yeah, kinda." Hannah shrugged. "Kiki, you're the image of your mom and Mera's the image of your dad."

"It's nice to hear people say that we look like our parents. We love our parents—they're great. But our grandmother…" Mera looked over at Kiki.

"Yeah. We love her, but ever since she went on a no-technology craze, it's been… different."

Kiki and Mera's family seemed to be getting closer and closer. It sounded like their mom and grandmother were speaking—or yelling—in Italian and her father was shouting in French, which seemed to make their grandmother even more angry.

"And I thought our family fought a lot." Zoe said, almost regretting her statement, not wanting to remind Hannah of the bad times in their household after such a nice afternoon with good people that seemed to care about them. But before Zoe could worry too much, Hannah nodded in agreement.

"Sorry, but we really gotta go." Kiki said as she took her sister's hand. "Thanks for the wonderful afternoon. Bye!" Kiki said as she dragged Mera away.

"Bye!" Mera called out before they got too far.

Hannah, Zoe, and Jack waved goodbye, but not as vigorously. They didn't want to attract the attention of the arguing family—especially as the disagreement got more and more intense.

After what seemed like a bit of explaining, Kiki and her family headed in the opposite direction, back the way they had come.

Jack walked Hannah and Zoe home, but left them at the end of the driveway, at Hannah's insistence. She didn't want him to have to walk them all the way up—and back down the driveway to the road after all the walking they'd already done today.

As Hannah and Kiki walked up the driveway, they both looked over at the cemetery, neither saying a word until they entered the house.

"Now what?" Zoe asked.

"We do what we always do around our family since your accident." Hannah paused, remembering the times that it felt like just the two of them and how those times disappeared once they moved to New York. "Play dumb."

"Hey mom." Hannah said as she and Zoe walked into the kitchen.

"Hey girls, the movers got all your stuff into your rooms. I had them set it up the way I thought you might like it, but feel free to change whatever you want."

"They were quick." Zoe said as the landline began to ring in the distance.

"I'll go get that." Martha left the kitchen, going past the girls.

"Zoe, do you trust me?" Hannah asked.

"Yeah, I always have and always will." Zoe replied,

which was true in more ways than one. Zoe hadn't always thought Hannah could have believed all the stuff that was happening to her, but she always had.

"You promise?" Hannah asked.

"Of course, why?" Zoe asked, growing more curious by the second.

"Just stay quiet and don't move." Hannah said as she walked over to the counter and picked up a cheese grater.

Hannah turned back to Zoe with the cheese grater in her hand. Zoe looked worried, but before she could stop her, Hannah pressed the cheese grater against her arm and slid it down her arm.

Zoe started to lunge forward to help her sister, but stopped herself when she saw what was actually happening.

When Hannah stopped and lifted the cheese grater, all there was on her arm were faint marks from her pressing on her arm. No cuts. No scratches. No blood.

"And I was pressing hard." Hannah told her.

"You know you didn't have to prove anything to me."

"I know. I just wanted to make sure that it wasn't a fluke—or my imagination." Hannah explained.

"A little risky, don't you think?

Hannah laughed. "Yeah, I guess it was." She hadn't really thought about what she was doing. Then again, she hadn't really wanted to think about the consequences about what she was doing. Otherwise she might have stopped herself.

"There is something happening to us, I know it." Hannah told her sister. "The strength, my skin, both of us hearing things." Hannah whispered the last part so quietly, no one else could have heard it—if there had been someone else in the room. Which there wasn't. But... just in case.

"Yeah." Zoe said quietly, but before she could get anything else out, their mom walked in.

Before their mother could notice what Hannah was doing and ask about it, she dropped the grater on the island and crossed her arms, smiling her most innocent smile.

"Why don't you girls set the table, then go see how your rooms look and put things how you want them." Martha suggested.

"Okay." Hannah was quick to agree. She and Zoe grabbed four plates, four forks, four knives, four cloth napkins which must have just been unpacked from the things the movers had brought.

Zoe and Hannah set their bags down in chairs, then set four places at the table as quickly as possible. Then they picked up their bags and headed up to their rooms.

"I still can't believe we picked rooms right next to each other—and not on purpose." Zoe told her sister as they rounded the corner of the hallway that their rooms were in. She sounded as excited as Hannah felt.

"Yeah. What are the odds?" Hannah said, not really expecting an answer.

No matter how much she thought about it, it really was ironic. They had shared a hallway in New York, but that had been because there were only four bedrooms in the apartment—not because they had somehow instinctively chosen to be close to each other.

Since they hadn't been all that close in New York, it was even more ironic... that moving here had somehow bonded them in a way that the big city could never do.

"How did mom know where your room is?" Hannah asked. "She sent us off to pick rooms, but she never asked me which one I picked. Did she ask you?"

"Nope. She walked me to my room after dinner last night. We were talking about my birthday. Twelve may not be as big as thirteen, but it's special since it's my first birthday since we moved here." Zoe said.

"Yeah, I can understand why that would make it special." Hannah agreed.

"You wanna see my room?" Hannah asked.

"Sure." Zoe said as she followed Hannah into her room.

The furniture was set against the far wall and the boxes of clothes made the room even more of a mess. Clearly, the movers thought Hannah was just like so many of the teenagers she'd met in New York... a mess.

She sighed. It would take a lot of work to move everything around, but she could do it.

EXHAUSTION

Hannah and Zoe slumped against the door and slid down until they were on the floor, resting from all the heavy lifting and carrying.

They'd fixed Hannah's room first because they happened to be in there when they started. Then they'd worked on Zoe's.

In Hannah's room, the bed now sat in the middle of the left wall of the room, facing the right side of the room. Hannah's wood desk sat two feet away from the door, and her dresser sat across the room against the right wall with her full length mirror in between the dresser and her walk-in-closet.

Another desk—one that had already been in the room—still sat in the corner. The last piece they'd placed was a cube organizer, one with nine cubes, against the wall.

In Zoe's room, her bed was against the wall across from the door, next to the glass door that led to her balcony, with a nightstand in between. Her dresser was across from the bed, with her full length mirror next to it and Zoe's desk was up against the middle of the wall to the left of her door.

The rest of the wall her bed was up against and the wall to the right of the doorway was covered by bookshelves, soon to be filled with Zoe's knick knacks and her personal library.

All that was left for both girls now was getting all of their clothes, books, and knick knacks in place.

Zoe let out a deep breath as the door began nudging

against her.

Hannah searched for the strength to get up. She held her foot against the door to prevent it from opening. Then she helped her sister up before the door could open and knock into her.

When they were both clear, Hannah pulled her foot back and the door opened to reveal Ryan.

"Hey guys." Ryan said innocently.

"Ryan." Hannah whined from pain, not only from her body, but because she could tell he was about to cause trouble for her and Zoe. He always did.

"What?" Ryan asked, as if he was innocent and could do no wrong.

"Knock first, kay." Zoe said.

"No thanks." Ryan said. "Sick room." Ryan said as he walked past Hannah and Zoe and walked into Hannah's room.

"That wasn't a request." Zoe muttered to herself.

Hannah shot her a look, telling her not to let Ryan get underneath her skin so quickly.

"I should've gotten this room." Ryan said.

Hannah forced herself not to release a sarcastic comment, but an eye roll escaped.

"Can I have it?" Ryan asked.

"No." Hannah said as she walked over to Ryan.

"Fine." Ryan said, shrugging as he walked over to Hannah's desk. He grabbed a small pumpkin pencil sharpener, and started to run but Zoe stopped him at the door.

"Really, that's what you came in here for... to take something of Hannah's?" Zoe asked.

"To annoy us." Hannah stated the obvious.

"And to tell you that dinner's ready." Ryan said innocently, looking smug at the same time.

Zoe took the pumpkin pencil sharpener and handed it back to Hannah.

Ryan pulled out of Zoe's grasp and walked quickly out of Hannah's room. Hannah and Zoe followed him, mostly for the sake of dinner, but it was good they had.

"Let's see what's in here." Ryan said as he jiggled the knob to Zoe's room. When the door didn't budge, he stopped and turned back to Hannah and Zoe. "Your room?"

"Yeah." Zoe said as she crossed her arms and leaned against the wall.

"Why is it locked?" Ryan whined, and he sounded like a much younger child than he was.

"Because I don't want you going in there messing with my stuff." Zoe explained.

"That's a good idea, I should lock my door." Hannah said to her sister, who was patronizing her brother.

"Yeah, you should." Zoe agreed at Ryan's expense.

"I will find a way in there, mark my words." Ryan pointed his index finger at Hannah and Zoe.

"Yeah, yeah, yeah. Go find your way to dinner." Hannah said with a laugh as she gave him a little push down the hallway.

Zoe followed.

Downstairs, their mom had already put the food on the table.

Zoe and Ryan sat down at the table, Martha sat at the head of the table, Ryan sat to her right, Zoe sat a chair down from the head leaving a seat open for Hannah.

"What do you guys want to drink?" Hannah asked,

with a little smile. For just a second, she felt like a normal girl. Not the girl from New York, going from party to party, wearing all the crazy fashions, having her hair just right. But also not a girl that worried about weird dreams, or voices that call in the night. Just a normal girl asking her family what they wanted to drink.

A moment later, the feeling was overtaken by a smell —and that smell made the second feel like a thousand. Her nose was filled with a dozen scents all mixed up together. Trees. Grass. Old books. The different smells mixed together to form something different. This smell comforted her. So much so, she couldn't help closing her eyes and breathing the scent deeper into her lungs.

Then as her body warmed she almost heard a voice singing in her ears, but then the smell was gone and Hannah's eyes opened. With the comfort gone, all she was left with was her family and the smell of dinner.

A long second passed while she tried to adjust to the shift in her experience and intensity of the moment. Taking a deep breath, she tried to push the memory of the smell to the back of her mind, to focus on this moment.

"Everyone want their usual?" Hannah tried not to draw attention to her momentary distraction.

Martha and Zoe nodded, while Ryan decided to be difficult. "Whiskey, please."

Martha scolded her son. "Orange juice it is for you."

Hannah turned and left, hearing Zoe's voice before she got out of earshot. "At least he said please."

Hannah smiled. It wasn't quite so foreign anymore.

She got two containers out of the fridge. One pitcher of iced sweet tea and one of orange juice. Hannah poured iced sweet tea in two cups, and orange juice in one. After she put the drinks away she got into the freezer and filled another cup half full of ice and then went to the sink and filled it with water.

The smell was there again, but just out of range. The memory floated back to the front of her thoughts, but Hannah shoved it away, flipped her hair off of her shoulder and carefully carried the drinks into the dining room.

She gave Ryan his drink, then mom's drink to her, then Zoe's. Then she sat her own drink down by her seat and she sat down between Zoe and Martha.

"So, how was the town? Were the people nice?"

"It was wonderful." Hannah answered. "Kiki and Jack showed us the library, the local bookstore, a burger restaurant, the park, the local magic store, and the grocery store. They even showed us where the high school and middle school are. And everyone in town that we met was really nice."

"Wow, so you guys got the whole town." Martha marveled at her daughters morning.

Ryan rolled his eyes.

"Except the bad parts of town or any clubs. And the park, we didn't get to see any of the park." Zoe said.

"I see." Martha looked regretful.

"But we didn't really have an opportunity to see it, with Kiki and Mera's grandmother ranting and yelling up and down the street."

"Really?" Martha paused as if she had missed something. "Who's Mera?" she asked.

"Kiki's sister. She introduced us to her today." Hannah explained.

And at Martha's interest, they explained why Kiki and Mera's grandmother was yelling in *Italian* up and down the streets of Shadowhill, while they filled their plates and began to eat.

"So, you like the town?" Martha almost seemed nervous to ask, even though she had asked again and again. Perhaps she was just waiting for a negative answer beside Ryan's. So far she wouldn't get it.

"Yeah I do." Zoe answered.

"Hannah?" Martha looked at Hannah.

Hannah looked at her mother and hummed a little questioning sound, not realizing that her mother had been speaking to her.

"Do you like the town?" Martha asked once more.

"Oh. Yes." Hannah said with a big smile on her face.

"Hmm. I haven't seen you smile in such a long time, sweetie. It's good to see your smile again."

Hannah looked back at her plate and kept her smile, not wanting it to fade. Her mother was happy and that made Hannah happy.

Somehow Hannah and Zoe managed to get through dinner without thinking about their secret lives.

After a long, but comfortable dinner together, Hannah

and Zoe escaped and headed upstairs. Hannah went past Zoe and into her room, looking down the hall to make sure Ryan wasn't watching. Then she reached up and slid the key off the top of the doorframe and unlocked the door. Before they'd moved here, Martha had all the locks changed, but after she found out which room was Zoe's she'd given her the key.

Martha knew all too well the agony Ryan had caused Zoe in New York, sneaking into her room and tackling her to the ground, messing with her books *with dirty hands*... and leaving them on the floor.

Not to mention all the trash he usually brought in with him—and then he would leave it on her bed or her desk. Zoe would almost always have to vacuum her room after he was in there, because he would track in mud.

But all of that shouldn't be a problem here, with her being able to lock her room.

Zoe went into her room, closing and locking the door behind her. She laid the key on top of the doorframe on the other side and sighed. Before she could relax on her bed, she noticed a book sat there. It was at least three inches thick, a brown leather hardbound cover. The only decoration on it was a metal plate on the front with a crescent moon carved out of it.

She knew every book in her personal library. This

book was not among them. Recognition hit her and she backed up, expecting to find her desk. But when she went to sit, she only found the floor.

She looked back at the book. It was on her bed.

Why?

But most importantly how?

Had someone left it there? Her door had been locked. She got to her hands and knees and crawled toward her bed. Then she kneeled there, staring at it. She had read a lot of fiction, but she didn't think that this was the type of book to grow legs and just walk into her room.

Or is it?

She reached out and carefully touched it with her right hand. The leather was rigid, the metal wavy and cool to the touch. When she picked it up, that familiar musty smell wafted from the pages and soothed her. It wasn't something she was imagining then.

She looked out her balcony toward the cemetery and saw no one among the tombstones. She put the book back on her bed and turned away from it, went to the door, unlocked it without the key and left. Going to Hannah's door, she knocked.

"Hannah!" Zoe didn't even bother trying to lower her

voice. She was somewhere between terrified and at peace. Something weird was going on — and she had no idea how to figure out which it was. She needed her big sister... especially since Hannah had told her she was extra strong now. That strength might be just what they needed.

Not a second later, she heard feet rushing to the door and then the door flew open. Zoe motioned for Hannah to follow her and then took off toward her room. Hannah closed her bedroom door and followed Zoe, closing her door behind them.

Zoe showed her the book. "It looks like your necklace." Zoe told her.

Hannah looked over the book for a few seconds — and then she pulled the necklace out from underneath her shirt and compared it with the symbol on the cover. It was definitely a match.

So, her necklace had come from the same place as this book.

"Where did you find this?" She asked.

"It was just sitting on my bed." Zoe set the book back down on her bed.

They both stared at it, not sure what to think. After what seemed like forever, Zoe hesitantly opened the book and Hannah watched her. She wasn't really ready to see what was in this mystery book. There were too many things happening. Too many things changing. It was all happening too fast.

Zoe opened it to a table of contents, although the words were in a language that neither of them understood. Hannah grabbed Zoe's wrist, somehow frightened for her to turn the first page. Zoe looked up at Hannah.

"Can we look at it tomorrow?"

Zoe looked at her sister. Her face was pale, nervous. Hannah may have told Zoe about everything that was going on with her, but she was fairly certain this was not what Hannah was planning for her life when they moved to Shadowhill.

"Sure." Zoe said.

Hannah let go of her wrist. "Okay. I'll see you in the morning."

"Yeah. See you in the morning." Zoe said.

And then Hannah was gone, most likely back into her room. Maybe even trying to forget about the book.

Zoe knew... somehow... that she was about to go down a path with Hannah, a path neither of them had been expecting. The only way they would be able to fight their way back up would be together…

But would Hannah let Zoe in?

A VOICE COMES A... WAKING

September 16th, 2018

"Hannah." Hannah opened her eyes, she looked at her watch, pressing the glow in the dark button, forgetting momentarily about her new vision until the brightness burned her eyes.

Her watch read *3:15 a.m.*

"Hannah." The voice whispered again. At least it sounded like it was the woman—not the man from her dream.

"Hannah." She seemed to be losing whatever patience a disembodied voice could have.

Hannah closed her eyes and pinched herself to see if she was dreaming. She let out a hiss of breath from the pain of how hard she pinched without thinking about her new strength.

She opened her eyes... and waited... and waited for something—or maybe nothing—to happen.

"Hannah." She groaned. She wanted to go back to sleep, but the voice was unrelenting.

"Hannah!"

At that call, Hannah pulled off the covers and swung her legs over her bed and walked toward her door as the voice called again. She opened the door and walked out, closing the door behind her. Hannah started down the hall just as Zoe came out of her room and closed the door quietly, not noticing Hannah was standing right behind her. Hannah rolled her eyes.

"Zoe!" Hannah whisper-yelled, making Zoe jump. "What are you doing?"

"I'm following the voice." Zoe whispered back. "What are you doing?"

"I'm following the..." She stopped, certain she had heard her sister wrong. "Wait. You can hear the voice?"

"Of course I can hear the voice. Who couldn't hear the voice? It's really loud." Zoe argued, even while she answered.

Hannah crept closer to Zoe. "You can't follow the voice. I don't want you to get hurt."

Zoe did not relent. "I'll be fine, so I'm going." After a second, she added, "Why would I hear it if I'm not supposed to follow it?"

"I can't convince you not to, can I?" Hannah asked.

"No." Zoe said and then she stubbornly started down the hall with Hannah following close to her.

"I already checked to see if I was dreaming. Did you?" Zoe asked.

"Of all the things you ask me in this situation, that is not the most important thing to think about."

Zoe rolled her eyes and they continued to follow the voice.

"Of course I checked."

Zoe laughed a little at her sister's admission, but then stopped laughing as they passed Ryan's room.

Hannah and Zoe tiptoed through the house, through the halls, down the stairs, around corners and to the last hall. A gust of wind blew... Hannah grabbed Zoe's hand and pulled her closer. The voice sung their names. For the rest of the walk down the hall, Zoe held tightly to her sister's hand.

The closer they got to the voice, the closer and tighter Hannah held to Zoe. They turned the last corner and on their right, a door actually glowed.

Hannah gasped and wrapped her arms around Zoe, shielding her from the door. But Zoe shifted so they would both would be facing it—and it stopped glowing.

Hannah released her sister a little, but only a little, as the voice called to them again.

Hannah tried to push Zoe behind her, but Zoe took Hannah's hand. With her sister griping her hand, she felt courage surge through her body—only it felt like Zoe's courage was there with hers... taking over hers.

Hannah had never felt courage like this in her life. The only time she'd felt brave was during Zoe's accident and she'd only felt the type of bravery that came with being a big sister.

This courage felt borrowed, different, stronger even than her own.

She squared her shoulders—and then before the courage could slip away, Hannah reached out and opened the door.

Nothing came out. Not a ghost. Not a monster.

The voice called, and with the voice came a gust of wind from the other side of the door. On that other side, there were stairs. Down those stairs, it was dark, even to Hannah.

The basement. It must be.

Hannah headed in first, Zoe followed close behind.

The door shut behind them. They turned and looked at it. Complete darkness surrounded them. The voice called again.

"Hannah?" Zoe asked.

"Yeah?" Hannah looked up at her sister. Her vision had finally adjusted.

"We should probably keep going."

Hannah nodded, took a deep breath and continued down the stairs with Zoe following.

When they both got to the bottom of the stairs, the basement lit up from candles all around the room.

Zoe looked up the stairs, but there was no one there. No one had come in behind them. She looked around. There was no one there.

"I've got a weird feeling about this." Zoe said.

"Zoe." Their gazes met. "If you have a bad feeling, maybe just keep it to yourself." Hannah said.

Zoe answered. "It's weird, but it's not bad." A second later, as she looked at the wall to the right of the room and saw that the wall was covered in spiderwebs, she said her sister's name instead of the disembodied voice. "Hannah."

"My word you're starting to sound like the disembodied voice." Hannah said and looked where Zoe was looking.

When she saw what her sister was looking at, she shuddered a little. She could only hope they weren't about to discover a new species of spiders that liked to create entire walls of webs.

After a few seconds, the spiderwebs actually started glowing bluish white in the middle—and it slowly spread out to the four corners.

"That's not normal." Hannah's fear was speaking as she put her arm in front of Zoe, backing up them both.

"No, it isn't." Zoe sounded more curious than afraid, which confounded Hannah the most.

All Hannah could think was *How could someone not be afraid in this situation?*

A gust of cold wind blew toward them from beyond the wall of spiderwebs. Somehow, within the wall of webs, something was emerging. Not a spider, thankfully. A shadow. It darkened in places, creating the image of a person.

The figure seemed far away at first, but they slowly got bigger and bigger until Hannah and Zoe could both see the figure was a woman. Somehow over the bluish tinge of the webs, Hannah and Zoe could still see different colors, light and dark, shadows, shapes, what it took to make a person;s shape.

The woman was truly beautiful. Not an ounce of makeup was anywhere on her. She had dark brown hair that reached her waist, brown eyes, a simple red dress that reached her feet, yet billowed in the wind that still blew against Hannah and Zoe. She was barefoot, just like Hannah and Zoe were. Zoe pushed her way forward to stand by Hannah's side.

Hannah put her arm in front of Zoe and tried to get in front of her, but Zoe remained at her side, Hannah realized that it was futile to try to stop her, so she lowered her arm a little. No use wasting her energy.

The woman stepped forward and it was like she was in the wall, but also, she was popped out as she would be if they were looking at a 3D screen. She was transparent. All they could see through her was more spider web. She turned her head to her right and her hair moved as if it was underwater.

Zoe mirrored her movement and tilted her head to her left.

"Hannah, Zoe." The ghost said. Hers was definitely the voice that had been calling them.

Hannah took a couple steps back, but Zoe remained, except for taking a few steps to her left... into the center of the room.

"You've finally come. Please don't be afraid, I will not hurt you." The woman said.

"What and who are you?" Hannah asked.

"My name is Amanda Hughes. You could call me a ghost of someone who once lived in this house." The woman answered.

"And you won't hurt us?" Hannah asked.

"No, never." Amanda said.

Hannah walked forward to stand next to her sister. "What do you want, why did you call us here?" Hannah asked.

"Your destinies." Amanda answered. "This is the reason I'm here. I am meant to tell you about your destinies." She went on.

"What do you mean?" Zoe asked.

"Yeah, what destinies? We didn't order any destinies!" Hannah said.

"Hannah." Amanda's voice had turned motherly. "You have already gained your abilities. This is your destiny, your powers will fill your life and you are destined..."

Hannah cut her off. "For what "greatness?"

Zoe shot her a look.

Hannah put her hands on her hips, her emotions building up faster and faster.

Amanda seemed to take a deep breath and release it. Hannah wasn't sure how that worked with a ghost. Maybe it was just habit. If she used to be a person...

"You are destined to save countless lives." She told Hannah. "You are a *Protector*."

Zoe looked back at Amanda. "What are her abilities? All of them?" Zoe asked.

Hannah looked at Zoe, crossing her arms, perplexed and dumbstruck by her sister's lack of worry.

"Her senses have been heightened. Her strength has increased considerably. Her skin has become like diamonds. You will find that it will be nearly impossible for enemies to cut you—and, should you get hurt, your healing will be considerably faster than any human." Amanda explained.

Amanda and Zoe stared at Hannah, while she stared into space, soaking up the information.

Zoe started to look away.

"Wait!" Zoe looked up at her sister when she spoke. "I didn't want powers, I don't know what you're talking about. I never asked for this!" Hannah said, her face contorted with confusion and a little anger.

"You were meant for them, Hannah." Amanda

explained.

"Why now that I'm here?" Hannah asked.

"Because this is your family's home, your great grandfather grew up here." Amanda answered.

"What?" Hannah's mind seemed to be clouding. She took a step toward the stairs, holding her head and staring off into space.

"Read the book underneath Zoe's bed. Then you will understand." Amanda said, taking a step back into the webs. Seconds later she was gone and the glow retracted to the middle of the wall before fading out. The candlelight blew out at the same time.

"Let's get outta here." Hannah said as she grabbed Zoe's hand and pulled her up the stairs and through the basement door. They heard the basement door close as they speed walked through the house and up the stairs and then on to Hannah's room.

She paced back and forth across her room. Zoe took the opportunity to go and get the book.

"What are you doing?" Hannah asked.

"I want to see what a Protector is, and Amanda said that we should read this book." Zoe said as she sat on Hannah's bed.

"Fine." Hannah said as she sat down next to Zoe.

Zoe searched through the book for answers. "I found something, would you like to hear it?" Zoe asked.

When Hannah didn't answer, Zoe asked again. "Do you want to hear it?" Zoe waited another few seconds, but with no answer from Hannah, she turned back to the book and began to read.

"Okay, a Protector is a person in a family who protects good people and defeats bad monsters. Apparently there are a lot of families that have the Protector gene. After a Protector dies, the abilities pass to another family down the line. The Protector gene can skip generations, but there will always be another."

"The Protector's abilities are exactly what Amanda described. It turns out that in the passing years, the families that carry the Protector gene are starting to thin. Not as many families have this gene anymore."

Zoe paused. This was fascinating to her. It was sort of like something that Zoe had wished would happen to her when they were living in New York.

"I guess that's you." She added, looking up at Hannah. Her eyes were wide, her mouth quivering and her breath was barely escaping.

"Hannah?" Zoe asked, worry filled her face, she wasn't sure what Hannah might do, scream, cry, run maybe? But Zoe was determined to be by her side no matter what.

A FEARFUL SOUL

"Hannah?" Zoe asked again.

Hannah hadn't moved in five whole agonizing minutes. "Hannah?" Zoe put her hand on Hannah's shoulder, closing the book.

"I don't..." Hannah said quietly almost like a whisper. "I can't be..." Hannah's words came out in a choking, broken sort of croak.

"Hannah, we can read some more, find out more,

229

where this came from, what to..."

"Get out." Hannah interrupted Zoe.

"What?" Zoe asked.

"Get out of my room, and take that book out of this house." Hannah pulled herself away from Zoe and tucked her legs up to her chest.

"Hannah." Zoe spoke softly, moving closer, trying to comfort her.

"Get out!" Hannah said sharply, staring hard at Zoe. Her eyes were full of anger, pain, denial but overall, filling her eyes... was fear. "Now!" Hannah said—and she was actually scaring Zoe a little now. Her tone was sharp, sounding like a thousand knives to Zoe's heart.

Zoe didn't say anything as she pulled the book to her chest, stood up and walked to Hannah's door. When she took hold of the doorknob, she turned back, but nothing came to her mind to say. After a moment she turned and left, closing the door behind her. She stood outside the door, waiting to think of something else she could say to her sister. After a few seconds, she heard the sound of rustling covers, and then Hannah's voice. It was muffled by the thick door, but Zoe leaned in a little, trying to catch what her sister was saying.

"Lies. I'm sure they were just lies." Seconds later the light in her room went out.

Zoe turned away and went back to her room. She put the book back under her bed and paced for about fifteen minutes, trying to figure out why her sister would lose her temper with her when Zoe hadn't done anything! It was not at all like Hannah.

No, they hadn't been super close in New York, but Hannah had never just been rude and mean to Zoe like that. What was it about finding out she had a destiny that would make her react that way? Especially since she had said she wanted answers for what was making these weird things happen to her. She had answers now, but she was angry about them, insisting they were lies.

Suddenly the weight of it all was too much for Zoe, and she stopped pacing, her body sagging from exhaustion. Maybe some sleep would help her make sense of it all. She could figure all of this out in the morning. She moved over to turn off the lamp on her desk—and then on her way to the bed, she looked out through the glass balcony doors and saw a dark figure lurking in the cemetery.

Tomorrow.

With a resigned sighed, she turned back to her bed and climbed in. She tossed and turned for awhile... and then finally drifted off to sleep.

The morning came quickly, but Zoe woke feeling so refreshed, it actually took her a minute to remember the events of the early morning. She sighed and undid the braid she had put her hair in before she'd gone to bed the first time last night. She shook out her hair and it curled down to her hips.

She sighed again and pulled off the covers, swung her legs over, got up and walked over to her balcony glass doors. She opened the right door and leaned against the doorframe, remembering the dark figure in the cemetery.

But when she focused in the cemetery she saw Hannah there—not some shadowy figure. She was digging a hole in with a shovel she must have found somewhere. After a few seconds, Zoe watched her drop something in the hole and then start covering it up.

Panic had Zoe rushing over to her bed. The book was still where she'd left it last night... this morning. That was when realization hit her.

Hannah was burying the necklace.

Zoe looked back at her sister, a cool breeze wafted through her hair. It felt comforting, familiar. She closed her eyes and enjoyed the cold air, until the memory of what had happened the previous evening wormed it's way back into Zoe's mind. She opened her eyes to see that Hannah was walking back to the house, with the shovel.

Zoe scrambled to her dresser, pulled out clothes and quickly got dressed. Today she wore jeans, dark green tennis shoes, and a dark orange short-sleeve shirt. Thinking of the cool air, she also grabbed her dark navy blue jacket and put it on.

Zoe ran her brush through her hair, and grabbed a stretchy hair band, so she could put her hair in a ponytail. She listened for her sister while she twisted her hair around and through the band.

A minute went by and then Zoe heard footsteps. She held her breath as the steps passed her door, stopped and then went into Hannah's room.

She slowly and quietly released her breath and opened her door carefully, making as little noise as she could and then tiptoed out into the hall. She rushed as quickly, but as quietly as she could down the hall. The farther away she got from Hannah, the safer she felt from an argument.

She knew that, after Hannah's blow up last night, she was not going to be agreeable. Zoe took the stairs slowly, knowing that she had a tendency to be a klutz when she didn't think about it. But then she tore out the front door, nearly slamming it closed behind her in her hurry—and ran to the cemetery. Normally she didn't like running, but it felt necessary in this situation. Zoe went through the gate and not far into the cemetery she saw a pile of freshly dug up dirt.

She squatted down beside the hole, rocking back on her heels as she looked back to make sure no one was watching her. After checking all of the windows near where she knew her room and Hannah's were, she started digging into the dirt with her fingers.

After a fair amount of digging, she found a white cloth. She swiped away the remaining dirt and pulled up the cloth. She could already feel the shape of the crescent moon through the cloth.

Zoe closed her eyes and an image flashed across her vision—behind her closed eyes... like a memory. Zoe was in the foyer, but there was carpet instead of the marble. She saw herself clutching the necklace and a note. She couldn't see what the note said, but she felt such powerful sadness, it was almost unbearable. So much so, she could feel a tear sliding down her cheek in the vision and then one was slipping down her cheek in the here and now.

Zoe opened her eyes, looked back to the cemetery and the white cloth in her right hand. She wiped away the tear with her arm, put the necklace and the cloth it was wrapped in aside and pushed the dirt back into place. She patted the dirt into the ground, then wiped her hands as clean as she could. Then she picked up the necklace and the cloth, stood and headed back to the house, closing the cemetery gate behind her, staring at the cloth the entire way back to her room.

When Zoe got back inside, she went to the bathroom at the end of the hall from her bed room. She washed her hands and then left, leaving the cloth in the hamper in the bathroom. She stared at the necklace in both her hands as she walked back to the bedroom, praying that she didn't run into her sister, literally. But she got back inside her room with no trouble and Hannah almost seemed non-existent as Zoe shut her door.

Zoe stared at the necklace, wondering how Hannah had come across it, and then wondering how Hannah could just toss away something that seemed meant for her. It wasn't often that something just appeared around your neck.

Zoe held it to her chest, another tear escaping. She could understand why the strange events would freak someone like Hannah out. She wanted so much to just be normal. Never to have to worry about life or death stuff.

Never have to worry about who to trust. Never have to worry about having monsters jumping out at you.

But Zoe was Hannah's opposite when it came to that. She'd always wanted a life of adventure. She had never wanted to be normal. She never wanted to be the average kid... or tween. She'd felt different all her life, but people had always treated her like everyone else.

Zoe felt that whenever someone looked at her they thought "Oh well. She's just another girl, we have plenty of those, plenty down the street and at the mall just like her." She'd always felt like people didn't even see her... not really her. She'd never really understood what was so great about being normal—why did her sister want so badly to be normal? She just couldn't wrap her head around it.

Who would want to be just another face in the crowd?

Zoe's phone chimed, snapping her out of her trance. She wiped her face and walked over to pick up her phone, praying that her sister hadn't texted her asking why she was in the cemetery this morning.

It was a relief to see that it was Kiki who had texted her. She'd forgotten in the midst of all the craziness that Kiki and Mera had exchanged phone numbers with them during the tour.

Kiki: "Hey, you and Hannah wanna get breakfast with me and Mera?"

Zoe laughed and smiled, Kiki's care was heartwarming. Zoe texted her back.

Zoe: "Love to, let me ask Hannah."

Just as Zoe sent her text, Kiki texted again almost immediately.

Kiki: "We're on our way to your place."

Zoe nodded her head absently and replied.

Zoe: "The door is unlocked, meet me in the foyer. See ya in a few."

Kiki: "See ya soon. <3"

Zoe smiled bigger. At least she felt like she could count on one person around here to be nice.

She sighed and figured she ought to get it over with. So, she turned, grabbed her black satchel that she used as her purse. It had been packed before, but she'd unpacked it the day before. She left her room and approached Hannah's door. Zoe knocked. Waited.

"Who is it?" Hannah asked.

Zoe knocked again, twice. Feet stomped toward the

door and it opened.

"Morning." Hannah said with a smile, as if she had forgotten their last interaction.

Zoe didn't smile, didn't shrug, didn't even move to come in when Hannah moved aside in an inviting manner.

"Kiki and Mera want to go to breakfast with us. I'm going and I told Kiki I'd ask if you wanted to come." Zoe said, her voice emotionless. She would put on her company behavior when she was with Kiki and Mera, but she could show how disappointed and hurt she was around Hannah.

"You know that sounds tempting, but I don't feel up to it. Maybe some other time." Hannah tried to sound like she was sad that she would be missing out, but Zoe saw through her.

She didn't say a word, nod or shrug. She just walked away. She walked right past her room, past all the other rooms. Just as she was about to turn the corner, Hannah stepped out into the hall.

"Zoe!" Hannah hollered but Zoe didn't stop or turn back. She just continued on, turned the corner, moving farther and farther from her sister.

Hannah didn't follow.

Zoe walked away alone. She was grateful for that because she really didn't want to argue. And she detested that Hannah was reverting back to the way she had been in New York, before their grandfather died.

Zoe came down the stairs and found Kiki and Mera in the foyer, looking up at the walls and ceiling. Mom had been hard at work, cleaning—so there was a lot more for them to appreciate now that everything was no longer covered in cobwebs and dust.

A smile crossed Zoe's face and so did her company face. Kiki noticed Zoe first, her face filled with joy when she saw her.

"Zoe!"

"Hi."

Mera turned and smiled, just as Martha entered from the hall that led to the kitchen.

"Good morning."

"Morning mom. You've met Kiki. This is her sister, Mera. They asked me to go to breakfast with them if that's okay." Zoe told her mother.

"Oh well. I think that's a great idea. It was very nice to

see you again, Kiki. Very nice to meet you, Mera." Martha said looking from Kiki to Mera and then back.

"Nice to see you again, Mrs. Autumn." Kiki said while Mera just nodded again. Zoe walked down the rest of the stairs and joined her friends.

"See you later mom." Zoe said as they started toward the front door.

"Love you!" Martha called.

"Love you mom!" Zoe looked back at her mom then up the stairs and then looked at her mom again. They exchanged smiles before Zoe followed her friends out of the house, closing the door behind her.

SEPARATED BY FEAR

"I'm sorry that Hannah didn't feel up to coming." Zoe said. She was walking in between Kiki and Mera down the driveway, with Kiki on her left, Mera in her right.

"Did you make her not feel good?" Mera asked.

Zoe looked at her... perplexed. That wasn't a question she heard often.

"No." Zoe said.

"Then you have nothing to apologize for." Mera said with a smile.

Zoe smiled back, it was nice to have people she could relate to.

"Was it something we did?" Kiki asked.

Zoe looked at Kiki. "No, she's just..." she grunted with frustration. "She's kinda in a mood." Zoe finished with a sympathetic "sorry" written across her face. Zoe looked down at the ground as Kiki and Mera looked at her with sympathy.

They turned out of the driveway onto Dreaming Tree Lane and Kiki and Mera both wrapped their arms around Zoe as they walked.

"Her loss." Mera said and they left it at that.

Kiki and Mera brought Zoe to Deanna's diner. They sat down at a table in the corner next to a window.

"Please get whatever you want. It's on me." Kiki said sweetly.

"Are you sure? I've got money." Zoe said.

"No, you've just moved here, you need to get settled in. Plus, this is my treat." Kiki said, smiling.

"Okay." Zoe opened the menu, wondering if Mera was as stubborn as her sister.

"What to get..." Mera mumbled, looking at her menu as a young woman came over to the table.

"Hello, what can I get for you?" The girl asked, she had brown hair with blonde highlights, she wore a cream short-sleeve shirt, jeans and a small white apron over her jeans, holding a pad and pencil in her hands.

"Hey Robin." Kiki said. "This is Zoe, she just moved here." Kiki said motioning to Zoe.

"Oh, you're Ray Matthew's granddaughter, right?" Robin asked.

"Yeah." Zoe answered, guessing that before he moved her grandfather must have been well known in this town.

"Well what can I get you?" Robin asked.

Zoe ordered scrambled eggs, sausage and sweet tea, Kiki and Mera ordered the same and then handed Robin their menus.

"Okay I'll be back with those soon." Robin said then went to the kitchen.

Zoe noticed Kiki and Mera exchanged unsure looks, like they wanted to talk about something, but weren't sure whether or not to bring it up.

"What?" Zoe asked after a foot was smacked underneath the table.

"Do you think your sister's gonna be okay?" Mera asked.

Kiki shot her a wide-eyed look. She seemed to think Mera was being too blunt.

Zoe took a deep breath and exhaled her words. "I don't know, she hasn't gotten upset like this since she lost her "best friend." Zoe said, using air quotes when she said friend.

"Oh." Kiki said.

"Do you fight a lot?" Kiki asked.

"Not really. In New York, we kinda went our separate ways. We only really interacted at home and the few times she would drag me to a party."

They both looked a little sad for Zoe.

"So she hasn't really been a sister for a while." Mera said.

"No." Zoe paused. Thinking over the last time Hannah was like a sister. "The last time we were sisters was a long time ago." Zoe paused, seeing if they wanted her to continue.

"Yeah?" Kiki sounded excited for a story.

"I was five years old, I hadn't yet turned six. And my family was living in New Orleans at the time. We were all swimming in this lake that we grew to love. Lake Rikersfield. My mom, Hannah and my dad were teaching my little brother Ryan how to swim and I was floating about twenty feet away from them.

They were in shallow water, but I wasn't. I was on a icicle pop shaped float and I was staring at the water went I felt something grab my leg and before I could say anything, it pulled me under. I yanked and pulled at the water, trying to swim up. The water was burning my lungs. I watched the sun fading.

No one was coming to save me. I looked down and saw a pair of green, glowing eyes staring at me. I screamed, letting go of any air I had in my lungs when I got pulled under. Then I looked back up and just when I thought I was about to pass out, I saw Hannah swimming toward me, deeper and deeper. I felt..." Zoe shifted so she could reach her right leg.

"I felt something scrape all the way down my ankle and then the hand was gone." Zoe pulled up her pant leg and revealed scars in the shape of five jagged claw marks.

They went all the way around her ankle and part of her foot.

"I started to swim up and Hannah helped me to the surface. She got me on top of the float so I could get the water out of my lungs. We swam to the shallow water, but never found out what tried to drown me." Zoe concluded her story and looked at Kiki and Mera, who were completely entranced by the story.

"Wow." Mera said.

"That's intense." Kiki said.

"Yeah, well that's my story… But enough about me. What about you guys? Do you ever fight?" Zoe asked.

"Oh we do, just not often, especially when our mom and grandma fight." Mera answered.

"Yeah, when our mom and grandmother fight, we try to get out of the house, and give them space." Kiki said.

"And when our dad gets into the fight, it's not pretty." Mera said.

"Yeah." Kiki said with her eyes wide.

Right then, Robin then came back with the drinks. "Three sweet teas." Robin said as she set them down and then left with a bounce in her step.

Zoe tasted her tea and then got three packets of sugar off the table and started putting them into her drink.

"You like extra sugar?" Kiki asked.

"Yeah. I've always liked my tea extra sweet. If it's too weird or something I can stop or leave and you don't have to talk to me again." Zoe said.

"No, no. Its a good kind of weird, we don't mind." Mera said. She was looking at Zoe like she couldn't believe what she was hearing, but in the best possible way... in a way no one else had before.

"Really? You're the first people to not mind. Besides my mom." Zoe said, looking a little sad. "Even Hannah thinks it's weird." Zoe added.

"Well then she's the one with the problem. Not you." Mera smiled.

"Yeah." Kiki smiled as well.

Zoe smiled, she hadn't known that there were actually people in this world that would just accept her the way she was.

TWENTY-ONE

TWO FRIENDLY HEARTS

Robin came back quickly with their food. She came, dropped it off, and left with a smile. Then she came right back to refill their drinks.

Zoe put more sugar in her tea. When she was pretty sure Robin wouldn't be coming back for a bit, Zoe pulled a cinnamon shaker out of her purse and started sprinkling cinnamon on her eggs.

"Do you put cinnamon and sugar on your eggs?" Kiki asked, staring at Zoe's plate.

"No, it's just cinnamon." Zoe said.

"Interesting." Kiki said.

"Can I try that?" Mera asked.

Zoe nodded, handing the shaker to Mera, who put some on her eggs and then tried it. She scooped some egg up, ate it and moaned.

"Hmm... That is good." Mera said and then offered the shaker to Kiki while Zoe smiled at them.

"No, no, I'm okay." Kiki said, waving the shaker away. Mera shrugged and proceeded to add a touch more cinnamon onto her eggs.

After they finished their food and drinks, Kiki paid. Then Zoe and Mera walked over together to the bookstore while Kiki ran over to the grocery store.

Mera and Zoe walked over to the fiction section and browsed until they saw Kiki outside. They walked out to meet Kiki, without buying a single book. Zoe was sad about it, but she didn't want to upset her new friends. Not everyone enjoyed spending hours in a bookstore or library.

"Got the cookies Grandmother likes."Kiki said, holding her plastic bag up.

"Thank goodness." Mera said, her right hand over her chest. "You want to come by the house now or after Grandma leaves?"

"Maybe after." Zoe said and they agreed that would be best. Zoe walked with Kiki and Mera back to Dreaming Tree Lane.

"You know if you guys live far from here, you don't have to walk me back." Zoe said.

"We don't mind." Mera said.

"No, in fact we live on this road as well." Kiki added.

"Oh, that's handy." Zoe said.

They didn't talk much on their way back to Zoe's driveway, but Zoe enjoyed just being with people that didn't judge her and liked her as a person. When they finally reached Zoe's driveway, no one seemed to want to part ways—which was kind of nice.

"Thank you so much for breakfast." Zoe said. Then she added, "And thanks for still wanting to hang out with me after I did crazy things with my tea and my eggs." Zoe smiled.

"Of course." Kiki said, returning a smile.

"And thank you for introducing me to cinnamon eggs."

Mera smiled.

"Oh yeah. I'm glad you liked them." Zoe said.

The three of them hugged and parted ways. Kiki and Mera heading back the way they came and Zoe heading up her driveway.

Zoe looked up and saw Hannah standing by the front door with her arms crossed and a very angry expression on her face.

What's she mad about now?

Zoe sighed and prepared for the storm.

TWENTY TWO

DIFFICULTY BETWEEN SISTERS

Zoe approached her new home with heavy feet. A confrontation was the last thing she wanted, especially knowing how stubborn Hannah could be.

"Where have you been?" Hannah asked when Zoe was a few feet from her

"Out." Zoe answered, avoiding Hannah's glare. "You know, going to breakfast with our new friends. The one you didn't want to go to."

"Why were you gone so long?" Hannah asked.

"I was hanging out with Kiki and Mera. Like you could have been if you hadn't gotten all weird over stuff." Zoe answered and tried to go in the house but Hannah stopped her.

"You know… why don't we just forget about the whole thing about Protectors and all of those lies, and just get on with our lives, okay?" Hannah suggested. Zoe sighed. This was it then—the big blow out.

"I don't want to forget, I'm going to get to the bottom of this, even if you're too scared to." Zoe said, trying to remain calm.

"Scared?" Hannah asked. "You're calling me scared?"

"Yes, I am. You just want to be like every single other girl, when you know that you *are* different, so you just push your differentness away and try to forget about it. Well, I ask you what's so great and amazing about being normal?" Zoe asked.

"Let's see, you get to go to school dances, graduation, jobs, birthdays, and people don't die supernatural and unexplained deaths." Hannah refuted. "And with my differences, there's lies, sneaking around, people dying left and right, not getting to go to school dances, and possibly graduation, not knowing who to trust, and being a freak, not having any friends." Hannah added.

"Also, being unique, not having something other girl or boys have, I'm not saying you're better than other people but you're different, so what if you can't go over to your so-called-best-friend's house and paint your nails and gossip about boys, if everyone was like everyone else it wouldn't be right, it would be the same thing over and over, every day, I wouldn't want to live in that world." Zoe said.

"But being different is lonely, I don't like being alone." Hannah said.

"You're one to talk." Zoe muttered under her breath.

"What?!" Hannah asked, her tone gaining a thousand knives like the night before.

"Well you're gonna be, because a lot of people don't just accept people like us into their lives. We'll be the ones that have to change. And I will never change for someone else." Zoe said, ignoring Hannah then started for the cemetery, but then stopping and turning back to Hannah.

"If you want, you can change to be the best friend to the most bratty, rich, fashion-obsessed girl in school. Fine. Just don't try to drag me down with you, let me live my life, and I'll let you live yours." Zoe said with tears in her eyes then speed-walked toward the cemetery.

Hannah followed her and grabbed Zoe's arm. "Zoe. Come on let's talk this through." Hannah said, keeping a firm grip on Zoe's arm.

"No!" Zoe shouted. "If you want the normal life that's your problem, not mine, you've done it without me before, you can do it again. Let me go!" Zoe said and Hannah's hand opened.

Judging by Hannah's expression, it seemed to open on its own.

Zoe backed away, turned and ran the rest of the way to the cemetery.

Hannah ran the opposite direction—into the house.

TWENTY THREE

A GUT FEELING

Zoe ran through the cemetery, and into the woods. She pushed past tree branches, jumped over fallen limbs. The farther she was from home, the farther away her problems seemed to get.

She ran into an open area in the forest, with the weeping willow and bench that Hannah had described. She tripped over a tree root and fell to the ground, leaves crunching under her knees.

"Ow." Zoe said. She put her hands down on the

ground, centering her balance. Ahead of her, leaves crunched. Zoe looked up toward the noise as a nervous ticking sunk into her stomach. More crunching came, then a low growling.

Zoe didn't know what to do. She sat there on the ground, hands and knees on the ground, sitting on her heels, while the growling grew louder.

A dark figure emerged from the forest a couple of yards in front of Zoe. She gasped and another figure flew over her head. She tucked her head down as the second figure tackled the first figure and Zoe cringed as the second figure drove a stake through the first dark figure's chest and it turned to dust.

Zoe looked away but heard nothing. She didn't move for what felt like a few minutes. She felt safe somehow, yet hesitant. When she finally fought off the fear, she looked up.

The man who had protected her was standing there... just a few feet away. He had spiky brown hair, and was dressed all in black.

She looked into his brown eyes. No alarm went off in her head, so he was obviously trustworthy.

Zoe's mother had always told her that she had a great knack for knowing who to trust and who not to trust. It was handy for a family who lived in New York.

"You. . ." Zoe said, just now realizing that it was him who had been in the cemetery outside their bedrooms.

The man walked over to Zoe and offered his hand to help her up, Zoe took it and stood up. He was very tall. Zoe had to look up at him. But then again, almost everyone was tall compared to her eleven... almost twelve... year-old height.

Zoe looked into his dark brown eyes and relaxed her shoulders. Then she looked down and realized that she was still holding his hand.

"I... I'm Zoe A-Autumn." She stuttered, taking the opportunity to shake his hand.

She still had a nervous ticking in her stomach that didn't seem to be going away soon.

"I'm Jared Callahan." He told her. "You don't have to be afraid." Jared's voice was soft. Maybe because he had just protected her from the monster—or maybe she was just crazy, but Jared's voice sounded almost brotherly to her.

"Okay. "Zoe said as she released his hand. A second later, she sighed. She'd just met him, yet there wasn't an ounce of mistrust that Zoe felt for him. She knew with her heart, he wouldn't hurt her.

Now to find out what exactly the thing was he had protected her from.

"Umm... What was that thing?" Zoe asked.

He looked away. He seemed indecisive on the subject. Maybe he was trying to decide between telling Zoe the truth or... lying.

"It was a vampire. Wasn't it." She didn't ask. She really didn't need to. She was pretty sure she was right, but she wanted to get his attention. She leaned forward, trying to make herself look a little taller or something.

He looked back at her. Part of him seemed surprised, but the other part of him didn't, that part of him seemed proud.

"Yeah. It was." Jared said.

"Okay." Zoe said as she soaked in all the information.

"How did you guess?" Jared asked.

"I know a lot about fiction. It wasn't hard to guess." Zoe said, not wanting to mention Hannah's dreams because she didn't want to bring up the argument they were having.

Jared seemed to recognize unease on Zoe's face. "Why don't you sit down." Jared motioned toward the stone bench.

Zoe nodded and followed his gesture. She sat on the side farthest from the way she came and Jared sat next to her.

A few minutes passed and Zoe realized that she hadn't said anything, she looked up at him.

"Who are you? If you don't mind my asking."

He sighed "Someone who has been fighting vampires for a long time." Jared said as he looked over at Zoe. "I'm here to make sure Hannah accepts her destiny." Jared said.

Zoe chuckled and gazed off in front of her. "Good luck, I've tried. She is determined that she doesn't want that life and she will probably do next to anything to make sure she doesn't follow that path." Zoe said.

"Yeah. I heard the argument." Jared said ominously.

"The one last night or the one today?" Zoe asked, looking back to Jared's face. She could see that he was impressed that she knew he'd been there last night.

He smiled. "Both."

"How exactly? You weren't anywhere near us. Not for either argument."

He shifted his weight, looked away and then looked back at her. "I have really good hearing." He said.

"Are you a Protector too?" Zoe asked. He looked away and laughed a little bit uncomfortably—as if she couldn't be further from the truth.

She stared at him and wondered for a minute if he was some form of vampire.

"I'm a Shifter." He said, looking back at her.

She shrugged and shook her head a little, not a hundred percent sure what he was talking about—though she thought she might have an idea.

"I can shape shift into a wolf. Not a werewolf, where someone turns into a half man, half wolf. But I turn into an actual wolf. A little bit bigger than an average wolf, but you get the point."

Zoe nodded, taking in the information. "Can you talk in your wolf form? I mean can you speak English?" Zoe asked.

"Yes. But I can also speak wolf." Jared said.

"Cool." Zoe said, looking off into the distance.

A few minutes passed without them saying anything.

"Thank you for saving me." Zoe looked back at Jared.

"Of course." Jared nodded, leaving his statement short.

Zoe thought she sensed that there was something he was thinking that he wasn't saying—maybe another reason for saving her... for revealing himself to her.

"To be honest, I was planning on coming to you tonight." Jared said, his gaze moving away from Zoe.

"Why?"

"We need to get Hannah to accept her abilities." He looked back at her, but Zoe looked away quickly.

"If she doesn't, so many people will suffer. Vampires and a various amount of enemies have detected that a new Protector has surfaced and they will be on their way here soon, if they are not already." Jared said.

"I've tried reason and I've tried talking to her. She won't listen." Zoe said.

"Is there a chance you would just try once more? If anyone can convince her, it's you. You're her sister, you have to know a way to make the evidence indisputable." Jared said.

He looked at her in a way that told her he was getting desperate. He was practically pleading with her with his eyes. "You're the only one I trust with this task." Jared added.

When that little tidbit sunk in, Zoe could see that he wasn't just blowing smoke. He really believed what he was saying. That made her feel more seen than she had been in her entire life. She didn't feel like Hannah Autumn's invisible sister anymore, she felt like a new person altogether. "You?… Trust me?" Zoe asked.

Jared nodded, looking perplexed at her disbelief.

Zoe looked away in surprise. Of all the things she'd expected of this day, this had not been on the list. "Why come to me? Why not just go to Hannah directly?" Zoe asked.

Jared stood there, thinking it over for a minute. "But wouldn't Hannah take it better from you? She doesn't even know me." She had to admit that he was correct. But she felt like there was still another reason.

Jared stood, looking like he might just leave, to go where, she didn't know. She called his name when he turned away from her—and he turned back to look at her.

She smiled. "How do I know that you aren't just using

me to get to Hannah's abilities?" She laughed after she said it, not really believing that he could possibly be using Zoe.

Jared smiled. "I wouldn't do that. And I get the feeling that you knew that before you even asked the question." Jared said.

"You're right." Zoe said.

Jared turned and walked toward the forest. "Don't stay in the forest too long. It's not safe out here." Jared told her. And then he disappeared into the trees.

But somehow Zoe felt like he would be watching until she went into the house. She sighed, stood and headed back toward the house.

She was pretty sure she knew what it would take to get Hannah to believe in her abilities. She knew that she would have to go down this road, dragging Hannah with her, or she might just lose her life.

STUBBORNNESS RUNS IN THE FAMILY

After closing the cemetery gate, a cold breeze blew against Zoe. She crossed her arms as she headed to her new home. With every step, Zoe stared at the mansion before her. She hadn't realized it before this moment, but she had already started to think of this place, this mansion, as her home.

It was ironic because she technically shared it with Hannah. Their grandfather had left it to both of them. Martha hadn't made a huge show of it around Ryan, but she'd told Hannah and Zoe that their grandfather had owned quite a few of the businesses in town as well—and he had left them all in Hannah's and Zoe's names.

Zoe wasn't sure why he left just about everything to her and Hannah, but she didn't talk about it much because she didn't want to bring up sad memories.

She walked through the front door and started up the outside steps, getting a few behind her before Hannah walked in from the hall where the kitchen was.

"Hey!" Hannah called from behind Zoe, who stopped just before taking another step on the stairs.

"What?" Zoe asked, her voice tired.

"We need to talk." Hannah said, climbing the stairs to where Zoe was standing, with her feet on two different steps.

"No we don't." Zoe said, turning toward Hannah.

"Yes we do." Hannah said, her voice seemingly optimistic

Well, maybe she's actually come to her senses without my help Zoe thought.

"I just don't want us to be angry with each other." Hannah said.

"Sure," Zoe said. "Just accept who you are."

"No!" Hannah said a little bit too loudly. "Those are lies, and you don't get to tell me how to live my life." Hannah added, returning to her normal voice.

So much for thinking she would come to her senses without me. Zoe thought.

"Yeah, but you still run from the things that make you different from other people, and welcome the things that make you alike, so I guess we really are different." Zoe said.

"It's not a bad thing." Hannah said almost whispering.

"No it's not, I get you not wanting to be different, alone, I almost get you wanting to be like other teenage girls, but what you are doing is tearing you apart. You were yourself after grandpa died, but now you are going back to your old self, the way you were with Maggie, and you don't care." Zoe said. "I guess we really aren't the close sisters I thought." Zoe added, then walked up the rest of the stairs.

Hannah followed saying "That is not true." They reached the top of the stairs and Hannah and Zoe speed-walked down the hall.

"Really, you may believe that but you don't…."

Zoe was interrupted by a ball hitting her in her face.

"Ryan!" Hannah scolded.

"I'm so sorry, sis." Ryan said coming to his doorway, He had hit Zoe with his soccer ball. "Are you okay?" Ryan asked.

"I'm fine." Zoe said, leaning down and picking up the ball. "Just don't play in the house, and don't even try to hide it just cuz we moved to a much bigger house." Zoe said as she handed Ryan his soccer ball back to him.

"Are you sure you're okay?" Hannah asked as Zoe walked away and started back down the hall.

"Oh yeah, just another day in Zoeville." Zoe said, not really caring anymore about the incident.

"Are you sure you don't need an ice pack?" Hannah asked, grabbing Zoe's arm.

"No, I'm fine! Just leave me alone." Zoe said as she yanked her arm out of Hannah's grip and started to walk away but then turned back. "If you want to go back to the sisters we used to be in New York, fine! But don't expect me to be happy for you. And I don't think Mera, Kiki and Jack will stand for it." Zoe said.

Then she walked away from Hannah and her brother. She walked back to her room and closed the door behind her, took off her dark navy blue jacket and plopped down on her bed. Tears threatened to spill over.

Remembering the way Hannah was before Grandpa died was almost too much. She hadn't been a bad person or anything. It was just that she'd ignored Zoe most of the time. She had spent most of her time on social media, not really making time for anyone else—kind of like their cousin Tilly.

Granted, she had her nose in books a lot, but Zoe had always made time for her family. She pushed her tears away, closed her eyes and curled into her bed. A faint sound of a little girl humming whispered in Zoe's ears. She opened her eyes and sat up, looking around, but the voice was gone. She watched the room for something curious to happen, but nothing did.

The rest of the day flew by for her. She mostly spaced out, going over her plan for that evening. Thinking it over again and again was making her even more nervous. The idea of it all scared her, but she had to do it. She couldn't figure out how, but somehow... deep down, she knew what Amanda and Jared said was true. Hannah was meant to save lives. Why else would she be given these abilities?

After dinner, Zoe went straight to bed, wanting to avoid Hannah as much as possible because Hannah hopefully would not start a fight in front of their mom and Ryan. And either Ryan hadn't noticed them fighting earlier or he didn't care to mention it to their mom, which Zoe was grateful for... either way. So, after a long day, Zoe put on her pajamas and snuggled into her bed and drifted off to sleep.

THAT COLD DARK FEELING

September 17th, 2018

Zoe looked around in the deep, dark, cold, seaweed colored water. Standing under the water, the surface dozens of feet above her... breathing in and out. And somehow she was standing and the sandy floor was miles below.

She looked up. She saw the sun coming in through the

water and the surface looked so far from her. That fear she had felt so often, filled her. She knew, if she looked down... she knew what would happen.

A tear came from her eye and it fell just as it would if she were above the surface, She wiped her tear away and took a deep breath and something then pulled violently on her right leg.

She yelped—and water filled her lungs. She tried to scream, hoping someone would hear her, but she was still being dragged down deeper into the dark water that felt like it had no bottom. It felt like real water now, as it filled her lungs. Her lungs burned for the feeling of air.

A feeling of loneliness overwhelmed her. She felt like no one was going to save her. No one cared that she was drowning. No one cared about her.

She felt dizzy. The world spun for a minute, then stopped. She looked up and saw the sun, but no one was diving in to save her, just like last time.

She looked down, to see the thing dragging her down deeper into the water, knowing that she was going to look at the thing that was killing her... And just like before, she saw two green, glowing eyes.

Then... just as she was about to pass out from the lack of oxygen, her lungs so heavy with water she couldn't do anything but sink further into the crushing blackness... she sat up.

She was in her bed. It was just a nightmare.

She looked over her room, expecting to see someone in there with her, but she was alone. She pulled her covers away, swung her legs over, stood and walked over to her glass doors. She sighed and opened the door, walking outside. She grabbed hold of the rail. Her chest felt heavy. It felt as if there was a dam in her lungs and there was only a tiniest crack, letting only a smidge of air in.

She stepped back and leaned forward, holding onto the railing and took several deep breaths. She'd had that dream ever since her accident. It had stopped for awhile when they'd lived in New York, when they saw their grandfather more. But now, it was coming back. It was all coming back.

The water, the darkness, the feelings, the eyes...

The loneliness.

She looked up at the moon and stepped closer to the bars, a tear slid down her right cheek.

"Why?" Zoe said quietly to herself>

Zoe then looked to her right and saw where the water ran past the cemetery in her backyard. She could feel the water filling her lungs and throat. She knew she was on land, nowhere near the water. But the feeling, the memories were so vivid. She could never forget the feeling of water in her lungs. She put her right hand on her throat, then looked away to her left. Usually, water didn't bother her much, but just after the dream, it took a long while for the feelings to go away.

After a few more minutes, standing there, looking at the scenery, trying to let go of the memories, she went back inside her room and slowly fell to her hands and knees... slowly, so her sister wouldn't hear her.

"Dear heavenly father, I'm not sure what to do, please tell me if my plan is in your plan, if I am meant to go through with this. Or if I am meant to let Hannah deal with her life without my interference. Help me please." Zoe prayed, holding her hands to her chest. "I trust that whatever you guide me to do, that it's in your plan and that it's best for all of us, so please help me, tell me what I should do. Amen." Zoe added.

"Zoe." Amanda whispered, Zoe looked up at her bedroom door and a voice in Zoe's head told her to go, another told her to stay, Zoe felt like God was telling her to go.

"Zoe." Amanda whispered again, she knew, God was telling her to go.

"Amanda." Zoe whispered, and stood up.

"Thank you." Zoe whispered and then snuck quietly out of her room.

SAVING HANNAH

Zoe closed her door as quietly as she could manage. Then she crept over to Hannah's door, twisted the knob, staying out of sight as she pushed the door open... also letting it creak as much as possible.

"Hannah." She tried to make her voice sound as ghostly as possible as she spoke. And then she turned and ran quietly down to the end of the hall.

She stood, watching for Hannah—clinging to the corner of the wall... hoping that Hannah would follow, and without seeing her in the process.

"Zoe." Amanda called.

Zoe waved the disembodied voice away—just as Hannah came out of her room. Zoe smiled and ran away from Hannah down the hall, turned the corner, rushed down the stairs. Hearing Hannah close behind her, Zoe flew out the front door, leaving it wide open and then ran toward the cemetery. She heard Hannah running behind her and slowed down only long enough to grab hold of the black fence around the cemetery—using it to help pull her faster.

She was gasping for breath. She was losing strength. She was in no shape for this kind of thing. Before doubt could fight its way back in, she heard Hannah come up behind her.

"What are you doing out here?" Hannah said, her voice hard, angry. She too was gasping for breath—which made Zoe feel a tiny bit better.

She turned to face Hannah. "Helping you."

"What?" Hannah said as if Zoe was speaking in tongues.

"You have to believe in yourself." Zoe said.

"No. I don't." Hannah said.

"You say that they're lies, but you haven't denied that you believe them." Zoe said.

"Because I don't have to deny them, I know they're not true." Hannah said, putting her left hand on her hip.

"You can deny it all you want, but the truth always has a way of coming out." Zoe said.

"Especially since you have a sister who doesn't let things go." Hannah said.

"Did you just accept it?" Zoe asked.

"No, of course not." Hannah answered.

"Then I guess we're doing this the hard way." Zoe shot back.

"There is no hard way, all you have to do is let this go and come back inside and go back to bed." Hannah said, turning back to the house.

"Not that easy." Zoe whispered, bracing herself, she let go of the fence and waited. She didn't have to wait long before she felt an arm around her waist and one on her neck. She let her breath shake when she spoke. "Hannah." Zoe said, her voice shaking.

"What now?" Hannah said as she turned around.

Hannah looked like she was shocked and scared at the same time. Zoe knew her plan was working. It had to...

TWENTY SEVEN

SAVING ZOE

Hannah was shaking with fear. No amount of courage could squelch the fear reverberating through her body and the intense nausea churning in her stomach.

She stared at her sister and the person behind her. He looked like a normal man, but with his mouth hanging open, his canine teeth were sharper than any human's could be, and his eyes glowed an unnatural grey, a color that reminded Hannah of pasty dead skin. With the fangs and the eyes, he looked completely inhuman.

"What is that?" Hannah asked.

"Hannah, you know what it is, come on." Zoe said.

Hannah was shocked at how her sister's voice was shaky, stern and calm at the same time.

Hannah felt like she would cry from the fear, her legs growing more numb the longer she stood there watching the monster get closer to hurting her sister.

"I. . . I…" Hannah stuttered, but before she could say anything else the monster punched Hannah in the nose and she went tumbling down to the ground. Then the monster grabbed Zoe by the waist, pulled her over the fence and took off with her, even as she struggled against him.

Hannah held her nose, trying to figure out if she was bleeding or just hurting. As she stood there, what had just happened started to sink in and Hannah realized she had to go after them. She was Zoe's only hope.

So she got to her feet, opened the fence gate and ran past tombstones, following the… somehow Hannah accepted that she was chasing a vampire, something that she wouldn't have thought even existed a few weeks ago. But here she was, chasing after this vampire who was holding her sister captive into the woods—most likely about to have her for a late night snack.

Zoe had almost been drowned. Then about a year later she'd been kidnapped. Hannah had vowed then and there... never again.

So, of course... she chased after them.

She jumped over bushes, fallen branches, tree roots, anything that could inhibit her from getting to her sister faster. The vampire swerved out of Hannah's sight. She had to stop and look all around to find Zoe.

The moon shone through the trees, illuminating their surroundings.

"ZOE!" Hannah screamed, desperation covering her fear of the vampire until the only fear she felt was the idea of maybe losing Zoe. She barely heard Zoe's groans, but she took off in that direction in search of Zoe.

Desperation, fear and a sprinkling of courage fueled her. Part of her wished that she had never gotten out of bed, that she just put in headphones and gone back to sleep, that she was not running through the woods after a Vampire that was gonna kill Zoe.

But the other part of her wanted to find her sister, tear her away from that monster and do whatever was necessary to protect her sister from that monster... whatever was necessary to make sure that beast didn't bother them again.

Hannah stopped just behind two vampires leaning over Zoe, who was on the ground, struggling to keep them away from her neck. She kicked, she groaned and scratched them, they only laughed, seeming to enjoy the experience, which only served to enrage Hannah.

She looked around for something to stab the beasts. She saw a broken tree branch that looked kind of sharp. Hoping that would work, she picked it up walked behind the vampire that had grabbed her sister and stabbed him in the back.

Hannah released the breath she'd been holding. If they hadn't known she was here before, they would now. Thankfully, the vampire she'd stabbed made a noise somewhere between a groan and a growl—just before turning to dust in between the two sisters.

Hannah panted, looking at the branch in her hand, no blood, no bodily fluids were on the branch. Just a little dust.

The other vampire let Zoe go and turned to face Hannah. She turned and faced the vampire. All the fear came flooding back in that moment, fear of this vampire, his teeth, his hands, his strength.

From the corner of her vision she could see that Zoe was moving away... not too far, but far enough not to be used as bait again. Hannah didn't wait. She figured why not get it over with. So, she stepped forward and plunged the branch into the middle of the Vampire's chest.

But he didn't turn to dust. Hannah waited as a malicious smiled creaked onto the vampire's face. She was shaking a little again—and her voice had gone hoarse. She whimpered but couldn't seem to get out a scream. The vampire took hold of the branch. Hannah took a step back as he pulled the branch out of its chest and broke it in two pieces, Hannah gasped and backed away more... and more—and, before she knew it, he punched her in the jaw.

She fell to the ground. Unfortunately, she stopped when her back hit, not having enough momentum to keep going or roll away. The vampire leapt on top of her and held her down, its hands like vise grips around her upper arms. Hannah struggled, but the monster's grip kept her hands from doing much damage. All she could really manage was to push against its chest with her hands, trying to keep it from getting close enough to bite her. Despite that, it started moving closer, leaning toward her neck, mouth open and ready to bite into the soft skin there.

When it jerked, its mouth snapping closed as it made a mousy grunt—and then turned to dust right of top of Hannah, she could only cough and sputter in the cloud of dust that was slowly settling over and around her.

Her hands flopped down on top of her chest as she coughed and then gasped for air, sitting up in an attempt to get out of the cloud of dust—taking in big, fast breaths. She looked up and saw Zoe standing over her, a branch in her hands, panting out of sync with Hannah.

"Are you okay?" Zoe asked.

Hannah just sat there for a minute, leaning back on her hands. She wasn't sure if her voice would make it through the block in her throat, but she tried anyway.

"I don't know." She was more than a little surprised that she could in fact speak—though her words did come out more than a little breathy.

Zoe stepped over to Hannah's side and collapsed next to her, still looking hard at her, the branch still clutched in her right hand.

"What about you?" Hannah didn't even think about the words before they came out.

"For now, I think I am." Zoe answered, her words sounding breathy as well. She sat up and held her knees to her chest.

Zoe's arms felt like noodles. She interlocked her two index fingers, taking some of the pressure off of them. She thought of Jared. She wondered if he was watching right now. He said he'd been sent here to make sure Hannah accepted her destiny. Part of her wanted to call out to him, see if he was close by. She hesitated because of Hannah. Struggling against two vampires for what had felt like forever and stabbing one in the back—literally— had been exhausting. Zoe watched her sister's breathing normalize, She tried to slow her own breathing, but she continued to pant quietly.

Hannah's arms probably didn't feel like noodles because of her new found strength. Her breathing was already returning to normal. She probably did not feel like she'd been run over by a truck. And she probably didn't have a dozen scratches stinging and burning where she'd been dragged against the ground and then thrashed around as she'd struggled not to let those monsters kill her before her big sister could come and save her.

Seconds turned to minutes and the minutes passing felt like hours, when a voice called their names. Zoe looked up toward the sky. Hannah looked to her left, toward the house. After a second call, the sisters looked at each other.

"I guess we should probably go talk to Amanda." Hannah said.

Zoe's eyebrows shot up. She had not expected Hannah to say that. "Okay."

Hannah got up so fast, it almost made Zoe dizzy. Then she reached down to Zoe, offering her a hand up. After another moment of making sure she had her balance, she took Hannah's hand and her sister pulled her up. Then they silently walked back to the house.

Oddly, Hannah felt no hesitation as she turned the knob on the basement door and walked in, heading down the stairs. Zoe followed, closing the door behind her. Just as the basement floor came into sight, the candles lit. Hannah stepped down the rest of the stairs in the light she didn't really need, though maybe Zoe did, and then walked to the middle of the room with her sister at her side.

They were facing the spider web wall and the blue glow spread to the four corners and Amanda instantly appeared in her 3D glowy way.

"Girls. You've come back. I was worried that you

wouldn't, after the way you ran away the first time we met. I am glad to see you back here." Amanda smiled. "Does this mean that you have accepted your abilities?" Amanda asked, staring at Hannah, her eyes soft but full of fear and hope.

Hannah looked over to Zoe and wrapped her arm around Zoe's slightly-wider-than-Hannah's waist and smiled. "Yes. Yes I do." Zoe looked at Hannah and smiled. Hannah knew she was thinking about how her plan had worked. "Zoe risked her life so that I would believe. I couldn't really deny it any more after seeing the lengths she went to, for believing in me." Hannah said and looked back to Amanda, who was beaming, her cheeks somehow a deep pink.

"Are you ready for what's coming?" Amanda asked in an ominous tone, looking at both of them.

Hannah looked at Zoe, who only looked at Amanda. "Yes. I am ready." She wasn't completely sure if she was or not, but she knew she would try. She was not about to let her sister down a second time... or take a chance on her going to such lengths again to get through to her. She let go of her sister's waist and took her hand instead.

"You will be in for a dangerous road." Amanda added.

"We'll be ready." Zoe said.

"Keep each other safe, watch each other's backs, trust each other." Amanda said. "Trust those that you feel good about, but only them." Amanda said, looking directly at Zoe, and then she disappeared into the spider webs.

Hannah and Zoe embraced as the candles went out and then headed back upstairs and went back to bed.

A MYSTERIOUS NEW FRIEND

Zoe woke up to the birds chirping outside her window. She sat up and rubbed the sleep out of her eyes, she pulled the sheets away and swung her legs over and onto the floor.

She sat up and stretched, groaning a little as her abused joints and muscles resisted. The strange feeling that she would have many more nights like this popped into her head and made her cringe a little.

Why couldn't she have gotten a little bit of Hannah's

resilience at least?

Cuz I'm not the protector. I'm not special at all.

The thought was sobering, but also a little depressing.

All her life, she had wanted something to happen to her—and it had, but not at all the way she'd wanted.

Oh well.

She stretched a little more—and something on her nightstand caught her attention. When she focused on it, she saw that there was a folded piece of paper sitting there. She picked up the paper and unfolded it. It had cursive on it reading.

Zoe,
Meet me under the weeping willow.

Jared.

"Good morning to you too." Zoe said, folding up the paper and putting it in her drawer in the nightstand.

She got up, put on a gold sweater, blue jeans, and dark green tennis shoes, then ran her brush through her long curly, brown hair then headed downstairs.

She left the house and headed to the cemetery. When she opened the gate and went into the cemetery, she found herself looking all around. Jared had said the vampires only came out at night, but that didn't mean there weren't other monsters. Something about being out here... all alone in the middle of a cemetery made her feel weird.

She shook it off. She would have to get used to this — especially since this particular cemetery was in their yard.

As she walked, one of the tombstones caught her attention.

"Oh. You had a family?" Zoe knelt down in front of the stone. So many questions crept in to her mind.

"What happened to you, to your family?" She whispered.

"Something sad." Jared said from behind her.

Zoe turned and faced Jared. "How do you know?"

"Someone who… knew her, told me not too long ago." Jared answered.

"What happened to her family?" Zoe asked, looking back at the tombstone.

"Her son grew up, and her husband died a few months ago."

"Huh, something I have in common with a ghost." Zoe said, turning back to Jared. "I lost my grandfather a few months ago."

"I'm sorry to hear that." Jared said, his face and voice was sympathetic, but he didn't seemed surprised... almost like he already knew. Of course he knew. The whole town probably knew why they had suddenly moved here.

"It's okay, I've dealt with this for longer than one

would think." Zoe said, looking at the ground.

"What do you mean?"

"A few months before my grandfather died, I had a sick and horrible feeling that I was gonna lose him, one way or another." Zoe explained, looking up at Jared.

"That would be painful."

"I even told my grandfather and he told me not to stress about it. Then two weeks later, I found out that he was dead. So I guess I had a bit longer to mourn."

"Does Hannah know?"

"Hannah didn't take his death well, so I kept it to myself." Things were quiet for a minute or so.

"Hey! You believe me?" Zoe asked, Jared nodded his head. "Usually people don't believe me, why do you?"

Jared sighed. "I've had experiences with people that would have strong feelings about things, about people. The last time I didn't believe them, they ended up dead."

"So you have an incentive to believe me." Zoe said, her tone sad to think about Jared's past. Zoe looked away, keeping the air quiet, but Jared decided to break it.

"I knew him."

"Who?" Zoe asked.

"Your grandfather."

Zoe looked back to him. "What? How?"

"A couple of weeks before Ray passed, he came and found me in Virginia. I was dealing with a gang of vampires that was hunting Psyonics. After I staked the last vampire of the gang, your grandfather emerged from the shadows and told me…" Jared paused.

"What?" Zoe said, eager for the rest of the story.

"Zoe." Jared stepped closer to Zoe. "Your grandfather, Ray. He was your family's Protector, he had been retired for a long time. He told me that he thought his death would come soon and he told me that he was sure that one of his granddaughters would inherit his abilities. So he asked me to watch over you and Hannah when you moved here."

"He wasn't sure which one of you it would be but he was sure it was one of you. And he knew that your mom would want to move here after the divorce." Jared paused so Zoe could process this information.

She looked away, tears streaking down her face. "He knew about the divorce then?"

"It's my fault." Zoe quietly mourned.

"What?" Jared asked, taking a step closer to Zoe and putting his hands on her elbows.

"I told you. I told him that I had a feeling that he would die. I took away his hope." Zoe said and looked down.

"No, no, no. That's not it at all. He told me about your feeling, but he also told me that he was sick. And he told me to tell you that it wasn't your fault. If anything you gave him hope." Jared said as Zoe sniffled, looking up.

"How?" Zoe asked.

"Because he always worried about you and knowing how you were attuned with your feelings comforted him somehow. He didn't tell me why. You seemed to give him hope that you and Hannah would be okay. That was all he wanted." Jared gently wiped her tears away.

"You sure know how to comfort a girl." Zoe said and laughed a little. She hoped that Jared wouldn't mind, but didn't take time for doubt to creep into her mind before pulling him into a hug. Jared's chin barely touched the top of her head.

Zoe had never had a hug like this. Whenever she hugged Ryan, he seemed annoyed, and her father's hugs had always felt forced. Her grandfather's hugs had felt loving, but distant. This hug felt like two siblings who had been separated by an extended period of time and were thrilled to see each other.

After another few moments, they both stepped back and Zoe wiped the rest of her tears away. "He told you about the divorce?"

"Yeah, he knew that his daughter wasn't happy. He didn't think that she had been happy for a while. He told me that your parents told him about the divorce because they were trying to figure out a way to tell you and your siblings." Jared said.

"Yeah. That sounds like a good reason to tell Grandpa."Zoe said.

"So what did you want to talk to me about?" Zoe asked.

"I just wanted to congratulate you on your master plan. From what I saw, she can't really deny it." Jared said.

"Yeah. She told me that after seeing the lengths that I would go to get her to believe, she couldn't really deny it anymore." Zoe smiled.

"It was truly genius." Jared said.

"Thanks." Zoe smiled, swaying back and forth.

"No." Zoe looked dumbfounded by his single word. "Thank you for helping me. I couldn't have done it without you." Jared said.

"Of course." Zoe shrugged just as her phone rang. She pulled out her phone and looked at the caller ID.

"It's Hannah." Zoe said.

Jared shifted his weight, started to slowly walk away. Zoe grabbed his arm to keep him from disappearing like last time.

"Stay. Hey Hannah." Zoe said, smiling, not letting go of Jared.

"Where are you! You're not in your room or the basement, I've been worried sick." Hannah said, frantically.

"Hannah, I'm fine. I'm outside in the cemetery." Zoe said in a comforting tone.

"Why are you in the cemetery?" Hannah asked.

Zoe looked over at Jared and smiled. "You should come, alone, there's someone you should meet."

"Okay, I'm on my way."

Zoe hung up her phone, put it away, let go of Jared's

arm and turned to face him.

"What?" Jared asked.

"Why do you disappear whenever I talk to Hannah?" Zoe asked, slightly narrowing her eyes at him.

"I have my reasons." Jared said, looking at the ground.

"Sure, you can keep it to yourself a bit longer." Zoe said, then smiled.

Jared looked at Zoe, confused, then he was suspicious.

"Zoe." Hannah said as she walked up to the cemetery gate, Zoe walked back next to Jared, so she could face Hannah.

"I'd better not regret this." Jared said from between clenched teeth. It came out almost in a growl.

"You won't." Zoe said.

"Zoe, who is this, what's going on?" Hannah asked after she entered the cemetery and walked over to Zoe and Jared.

"This is Jared, he's the one we saw in the cemetery a few days ago." Zoe said, motioning toward him.

"Nice to meet you, I'm Hannah." Hannah said, holding her hand out to shake his hand.

Jared shook Hannah's hand, his face the epitome of calm. No one would have suspected a thing unless they were Zoe. When he let go of her hand he backed away so that he was behind Zoe.

Zoe grabbed his hand, still looking at Hannah and smiling, making sure that he wasn't going to disappear on her.

"What's going on?" Hannah asked, suspiciously eyeing the hand holding and Zoe didn't bother explaining.

"You explain things so well." Zoe asked.

"Do I?" Jared said sarcastically.

"Go ahead." Zoe said, motioning to Hannah.

"Yesterday, I asked Zoe to help me get you to believe that you're…" Jared paused.

Hannah crossed her arms. "Inhuman, supernatural, special, different." Hannah suggested in a snarky tone.

"Yeah, you could say that." Jared said, snarling back at her.

"Why did you go to my sister, why didn't you come to me yourself?" Hannah asked.

"A stranger telling you that vampires, werewolves, and

shifters are real... oh yeah. That would've gone over well." Zoe said sarcastically and laughed.

"You're right." Hannah said, smiling and letting a small laugh escape.

"What is that?" Hannah said then walked in between Zoe and Jared, separating their hands and knelt down in front of a tombstone.

"That's Amanda." Hannah said.

Zoe and Jared turned to the tombstone, standing behind Hannah... Zoe on Hannah's right... Jared on Hannah's left.

"Yeah, I saw that this morning." Zoe said.

"She's in our cemetery." Hannah said. "Did she die here?" Hannah asked.

"Possible." Zoe said with a shrug.

"Zoe." Hannah said.

"What?" Zoe asked. "She died, July 5th, 1958." Hannah said, her voice cracking.

"Oh my goodness, the same day as Grandpa." Zoe said.

"Sixty years apart, but yeah, the same day." Hannah

said.

"Do you think they're connected?" Zoe asked.

"I don't know, but this can't be a coincidence." Hannah said.

"I'm going to go down and talk to Amanda." Hannah said then stood up and walked toward the gate.

Zoe turned behind her and saw that Jared had disappeared again.

"Seriously." Zoe said, throwing her arms half way up in the air, she sighed then turned and followed Hannah into the house.

A DARK CONFRONTATION

"You don't understand, they have to know the truth! If I don't tell them, they may never know the truth!" Amanda argued.

"They don't need the truth, they have each other."

Paul had stooped so low, that he was arguing with a memory of a woman who had died over fifty years ago. Granted she had helped save his life, but he was dead now. That was the past. This was the now, where he wanted to live, but he shouldn't have to argue with a memory.

"Paul. I saved your life over fifty years ago from her, if she shows up in Shadowhill and she finds you alive, I won't be there to take a bullet for you and she will kill you. Don't you think that the girls deserve to know of her coming? Not to mention she will kill Hannah!"

"Why would she kill Hannah?" Paul asked. "She would be after me anyway."

"You know why she'd want her dead." Amanda said. "There is no reasoning with her, anyone who she doesn't like for whatever reason she has or anyone in her way, she doesn't care if they die, I would know."

"Yes, yes. I remember you taking that bullet for me, very noble of you. It's always the one who gets killed by the big bad that seems to know them so well, ironic."

Amanda crossed her arms. "You know I didn't have to take that bullet. You didn't have to live another seventeen years. I could have seen my son into adulthood."

"Oh please. If she hadn't killed you then, she would have found you and killed you and your son, just to hurt your beloved husband." Paul said.

"It's not my fault that my husband reminds her of her ex-lover from three hundred years ago." Amanda said, glaring at Paul.

Paul looked away, sighed and turned back to Amanda, who was getting on his nerves more and more.

"What about Zoe, Hannah's sister, wouldn't she want her dead?"

"No and you know this, she'd play with her, not kill her. She's not enough like him. You know I would know." Amanda said, motioning to herself.

"Fine, if they show up before midnight, you can tell them whatever you want, but at midnight you're gone." Paul said.

"Fine! You just want me out of the way, so you can go and try to do something stupid, oh wait. You don't have to try." Amanda smiled.

"So what?" Paul grimaced.

"So, Hannah will stop you, she's stronger than you think." Amanda said.

"What makes you so confident in her?" Paul asked

"Ray does." Amanda said.

A WILD TURN OF EVENTS

"Amanda!" Hannah called.

"Hannah, if you keep yelling, mom or Ryan may hear you and when they come down we'll be caught." Zoe said.

"Caught for what?" Ryan asked.

"Ryan, why must you eavesdrop?" Hannah asked.

"How else am I gonna find out your secrets?" Ryan said, his smile was the vision of an immature little brother that wanted to cause trouble. "By the way, breakfast is ready, and I'm gonna tell." Ryan said then ran up the stairs and ran off.

"Ryan!" Hannah said, running off after Ryan.

"Little brothers." Zoe sighed, rolling her eyes and shrugging. Then she started slowly up the stairs. Before she could get far, a breeze coming from the basement hit her. Zoe stopped and turned in the direction of the basement.

The faint noise of a girl singing was all she could hear. Zoe couldn't make out what she was singing because it was barely even a whisper of sound. She walked back down the stairs.

"Who are you?" Zoe asked aloud to the empty air and, as quickly as it came, the singing was gone and Zoe was left with only silence. She turned to leave, but kept watching the basement. "I'm here, when you need me."

She turned her head and headed back up the stairs. When she reached the top she closed the door behind her.

Zoe walked into the kitchen to hear Ryan in the midst of tattling on her and Hannah. "They're hiding stuff from us." Ryan said.

"Honey, your sisters have a right to privacy, just like you, and you should honor that like they do."

Hannah crossed her arms.

"But Mom." Ryan whined.

"Ryan, go set the table." Martha motioned toward the dining room.

Ryan huffed, but he gathered what he needed to set the table and stomped out the room.

Zoe's phone rang. "Hello?"

"Hey, it's Kiki."

"Hey Kiki."

"Jack, Mera and I were wondering if you and Hannah would like to go to a club tonight?"

"Let me ask Hannah." Zoe moved the phone away from her mouth. "Hannah, do you wanna go to a club tonight with Kiki, Mera, and Jack?"

"Sure, if it's okay with mom." Hannah looked over at their mom.

Martha nodded her head. "Sure. It sounds like fun."

Hannah and Zoe both smiled. Zoe moved the phone back to her mouth. "We're in… and both of us this time. We made up."

"Good to know, Mera was kinda worried." Kiki said.

Zoe smiled. "I've gotta go, breakfast is almost ready."

"Okay, we'll see you tonight."

"Kay, bye." Zoe said, then hung up.

Once breakfast was done, the girls helped clean and straighten the kitchen. They spent much of the day putting away their clothes and personal stuff in their rooms.

After dinner they headed up to their rooms to get ready for the outing with Kiki, Mera and Jack. Zoe picked out jeans, an orange long-sleeve shirt, her brown ankle boots, and she let her hair dangle down her back and shoulders and accented it with clip-on plastic flowers.

She put on clear shiny lip gloss, then put it in her purse. She checked to make sure she had everything she would need before she slipped the long strap over her head and let it rest on her shoulder.

Zoe left her room and went to Hannah's room. She

knocked on the door then entered the room and found Hannah sitting on her bed reading the Protector book.

"Hannah, you need to be getting ready." Zoe scolded.

"I know, but I just feel like I should be looking for something about you." Hannah said.

"You don't have to." Zoe said walking over to Hannah and closed the book in her lap, Hannah eyed her calm sister.

"I thought you wanted to be unique, supernatural, different." Hannah said.

"Who ever said I wasn't?" Zoe said with a slightly mischievous smile on her face, which made Hannah smile.

"I feel like if there's an explanation for me, there has to be one for you. Why you've always been a target, why weird things happen to you." Hannah said, getting up and going into her walk-in closet.

"Hannah. Just because I had a disease when I was a baby and I was kidnapped and I almost drowned under the age of ten doesn't mean I'm supernatural."

"I still wonder." Hannah said quietly.

"I know, so do I. Now get dressed, so we can have a fun night and relax."

"Okay." Hannah emerged wearing a light green shirt, khaki pants and black tennis shoes.

Zoe looked at her sister in shock. "No more dark clothing?"

"No. I figured it was time for a change." Hannah twirled once, giggling. She walked over to her dresser, opened the top drawer, looked around for a minute before pulling out a dark blue lip gloss and rubbing the gloss on her lips.

When she was satisfied, they headed for Hannah's door. "Could you put this in your purse?" She asked.

"Sure." Zoe said, taking the lipstick and putting it in her purse. They walked out of the room, down the halls and then down the stairs and out the front door.

Zoe sat down on the front porch. Not long after, Kiki, Jack, and Mera showed up walking up the long driveway. Zoe stood up, and they started walking to meet them.

"We keep this a secret, right?" Hannah whispered.

"If you mean the fact that we killed two vampires last night and that we will have to do it more?" Zoe whispered back.

"I will have to do it more." Hannah said, looking at

Zoe. "But yes."

"I agree." Zoe said just as they met up with their friends.

"Hey!" Mera called out to them.

"Hey." Zoe said

"Hi. It's so nice to see both of you." Kiki said sweetly. After hugging Mera, Zoe hugged Kiki then backed away next to Hannah.

"Let's go." Hannah said. They all walked to the end of the driveway and down Dreaming Tree Lane, then they turned left onto Main Street.

A NIGHT OUT ON THE TOWN

As a celebration of Hannah and Zoe talking to each other again, Kiki took them for ice cream. When they walked in, Hannah looked around the place. It was an ice cream store with about a dozen red plastic chairs, and a black and white checkered floor.

It wasn't a big room, but decent sized. It had a very old-fashioned look about it, which was very "in" right now, but Hannah had the feeling that what was "in" had nothing to do with the décor.

Kiki got chocolate chip cookie dough with a waffle cone. Jack got chocolate fudge in a waffle bowl. Mera got cookies and cream in a regular cone. Hannah got cookies and cream in a waffle cone. And Zoe got plain vanilla in a waffle cone. After Hannah got her ice cream, she glanced outside, and saw a dark figure standing outside across the street.

"Zoe." Hannah whispered, pulling Zoe over to her side. "Is that your friend Jared?"

"Probably." Zoe whispered.

"I feel like we should go over to him, talk to him... or something." Hannah whispered.

"About what?" Zoe asked. She had a tone.

Hannah wasn't sure what about, but it seemed like Zoe knew something Hannah didn't and she was trying to play innocent. She shot Zoe a look.

"I don't know." Hannah said, shaking her head and shrugging her shoulders. "Tonight was supposed to be calm."

"If you want to go say hi, go ahead, I'll stall." Zoe said, walking back over to Kiki, Mera and Jack. Hannah turned to follow Zoe, but then turned back to the window. The dark figure was gone.

The sun was gone when Hannah, Zoe, Kiki, Mera, and Jack left the ice cream store, still eating their ice cream and started walking through the bad part of town... ironically, at night.

"How dangerous is the bad part of town?" Zoe asked.

"Not that bad, just don't park your car in that area at night, especially unlocked, and you'll be fine." Kiki said and laughed quietly.

"What she means is that it's not that bad, they just call it 'the bad part of town' because a lot of homeless people hang out there and some of them can be creepy." Mera said, walking backwards while facing Zoe. But after a minute, she turned back and walked forward.

"Totally not confusing." Zoe said.

"Or safe." Hannah said, then took another lick of her ice cream.

Kiki, Mera and Jack led Hannah and Zoe to the club. The alley had only a few lamp posts, so the light in the alley was dimmed. They passed a few buildings before they reached the club. They had to go past the club to get into the line.

There were six people in line ahead of them. Kiki and Jack got in the line first, then Mera planted herself behind them with Hannah and Zoe behind her. She turned around to talk with Zoe about a book series that Hannah wasn't interested in, so she was only half listening to their conversation.

The line got shorter pretty fast. The bouncer let them in one by one. He had a shaved head, somewhat rough looking face, dark brown skin and kind, dark brown eyes. He wore black clothes and shoes, and had the build of a wrestler.

Hannah worried that he might not let Zoe in, but Kiki had reassured Hannah earlier that they let anyone in — and she was right. The bouncer let them pass with no trouble.

The club was big — two levels, judging from the stairs they passed just inside. The music playing was catchy and sounded like what was popular with teens. The décor was not unlike some she had seen in clubs she and Maggie had been to in New York. It was surprising in so many ways. The whole place seemed more like something you might find in a city — not a tiny town like this one.

Tables were scattered all over the place. To the right of the dance floor were booths and couches surrounding the tables. To the left were more tables and across from them was the bar.

"Wow." Zoe said over the loud music that a band called "The Diamonds" was playing. "This is amazing."

"You should see it from the second floor." Mera said, motioning to the ceiling above the dance floor.

Hannah looked up and saw an opening over the dance floor, people were leaning over rails and looking down to the first floor. Some of them were holding drinks. Others were just leaning against the rails, and talking to people standing with them.

"Why don't we..?" Hannah asked, motioning toward the stairs.

"Sure." Kiki said and Jack immediately took the lead as everyone followed him up the stairs.

Jack, with Kiki right behind him, led them upstairs, with Zoe behind them, and Mera walking close behind Zoe, almost next to her. Hannah followed behind the group. They all walked over to the area overlooking the dance floor and found a spot that was unoccupied.

Zoe slowly danced in place to the music. Jack watched the floor below them. Mera and Kiki joined Zoe. Hannah watched the people on the first floor. She looked around for Jared, certain the chances of him being seen was slim.

She didn't know why, since she had just met this strange person, but for some reason she couldn't get him out of her head. She searched and searched, but never found him. Someone else caught her eye, a guy, from what Hannah could see. He had dark hair, and was wearing a dark brown shirt and jeans.

He wasn't Jared, but as Hannah watched him, she was certain there was something familiar about him... though she really didn't recognize him.

The guy looked up at her and she realized that she had been staring at him. She waved and smiled, trying to pass it all off casually. The guy walked away from the stage and disappeared from her view. She leaned over the slightest bit, but didn't see him.

She tried to put it out of her mind. She shook her head, trying to shake away any thoughts of the stranger. A minute later, someone tapped on Hannah's shoulder. She turned to her left and saw it was the guy she'd been staring at.

"Hello." Hannah said quietly, but loud enough for him to hear her.

"Hello." Something seemed off about him, but she just couldn't put her finger on it. Still... a nagging twinge in the pit of her stomach somehow felt directed at him. It was like that feeling you get when you're starting to get a cold, but there's nothing you can do about it.

"I noticed you and I thought I'd come and ask you to dance."

"Hannah?" Zoe had stopped dancing and had all of her attention centered on the guy.

Hannah looked over at Zoe and saw the concerned look on her face. Clearly she didn't trust him. For just a second she considered that Zoe might be just acting like an over-protective sister, but then she remembered the last time she hadn't paid attention to Zoe's warnings.

"No thank you, I'm here to hang out with my friends." Hannah said.

"If you change your mind, I'll be downstairs. If not, I'll just find another juicy morsel." The stranger's smile was malicious, almost like he was thinking of her as a meal.

Hannah would never understand men who did things like that, consider women as food to be eaten up. Granted Hannah had lived in New York—where she'd heard about a lot of bad dating situations—but it still repulsed her.

The stranger walked away and the twinge in Hannah's

stomach dissipated. She took a deep breath and turned back to look over at the dance floor. Zoe watched her. Hannah tried to put the experience out of her mind, but she saw the stranger dancing on the dance floor with a teen girl. Hannah felt sorry for her until she noticed what looked like blood on her neck.

Then she noticed that the girl was barely moving. He was holding her close to him and she was starting to flop forward. Then Hannah felt afraid for this girl. The stranger started leading her away from the crowd and out of the club, Hannah turned away from the dance floor and headed toward the stairs.

She knew now. She was going after a vampire.

UNITED IN TRUST

Hannah bursted out of the club looking for the vampire and the limp girl.

"If you're looking for the couple that just came out, they went that way." The bouncer said, pointing to an alley to the left.

"Thank you." Hannah nodded at the bouncer.

"You're welcome." He watched as Hannah took off running after the couple.

She could hear footsteps running behind her. Somehow she knew that it was Zoe coming after her, but she didn't stop. Didn't slow down. A girl's life was at stake. She stopped at the end of the alley and found them.

Zoe stopped so close to Hannah that she could practically feel her without Zoe touching her. Hannah pushed the annoyance away, so that she could focus on the civilian.

"Hey!"

The vampire looked at Hannah and smiled wickedly. He let the girl drop to the floor. She wasn't moving. Hannah worried that she was too late, but seeing her breathing eased her thoughts.

"Leave her alone." Hannah said through gritted teeth.

"Ah. Finally the Matthews line has a new protector." He paused at Hannah's surprised face. "This town hasn't had a proper toy in so long. Nice to see that the universe is finally paying through."

"What's going on?" Kiki asked as she, Mera and Jack came up from behind them.

"What are you doing here?" Hannah was keeping her attention on the monster in front of her.

"We came to see what you girls were running off for."

Jack said, putting a potato chip in his mouth.

"You need to leave—right now." Zoe looked at their three friends.

"No, let them stay. I could use a big meal." The vampire gloated.

Zoe turned her head toward him. "No one asked you."

"You're a monster." Hannah was getting angry.

"Little girl's right." The vampire taunted, then his eyes turned gray and his mouth opened to reveal his sharp canine teeth.

"That's not possible." Jack whimpered.

"Why must there always be an idiot who says 'that's not possible'... it makes me sick." The vampire muttered.

"Good, then maybe you could leave us alone." Mera suggested. To Hannah's ears she sounded like a naive child.

"That comment also makes me sick." The vampire paused, looking away.

Zoe stepped up beside her sister. Hannah knew that she wasn't gonna be able to stop her—so, she didn't even try.

"But not sick enough to spoil my dinner." The vampire insisted, looking from Mera to Kiki to Jack to Hannah to Zoe.

The vampire launched himself at Zoe, pulled her in front of him, holding her neck to shield himself.

Hannah moved over to her left and stood in front of Kiki, Mera and Jack, shielding them, grateful that she didn't hear anyone else in the alley with them. "Let her go!"

"I don't think so." The vampire sneered, then slowly leaned over to Zoe's neck and opened his mouth.

Hannah searched for something to stop him — something to kill him. She saw a wooden chair to her right and somehow knew the lore was right. She needed a wood stake.

She walked over to the chair, lifted it up, threw it down, and picked up a broken wood leg.

"Zoe!" Hannah yelled, just before she threw the broken chair leg. Fortunately, Zoe pulled her body to the right just enough for the chair leg to hit the vampire.

The monster let out half a groan as he lost his grip on Zoe. She rushed over to Hannah, who pushed Zoe behind her. Mera wrapped her arms protectively around

Zoe as the vampire backed up against the wall, holding his chest wound. He looked up at Hannah as he slid down to the ground.

"The new Protector. She's here." The vampire wheezed as he dissolved into dust.

Hannah walked over to where he had been standing, bent down and felt the ground, ran a finger over the spot where he'd just been. Nothing but dust remained. She stood up and turned to face Zoe, Mera, Kiki and Jack.

"What the heck is going on?" Kiki asked.

"Well." Zoe paused. "Want the full version or the nutshell?"

"What is going on?" Kiki asked, the pitch of her voice rising as she continued to panic.

"That is a long answer to an over complicated question." Zoe told her. Mera was still holding onto her.

Zoe wasn't sure if Mera was in shock or was scared of losing her, but she obviously wasn't scared of Zoe. She was holding too tightly for that.

"You just killed a guy! And then he turned into nothing!" Jack sounded completely frantic.

"Again, extremely complicated and it depends on your point of view." Zoe repeated.

"We should really talk somewhere private."

Zoe had a feeling that Mera might be the only one who wasn't going to be stubborn about accepting the truth.

"Good point." Hannah nodded her head as she walked between the group and started down the alley.

"I'm not going anywhere, until you explain what on earth is going on!" Jack demanded. Hannah and everyone else just looked at him.

"Jack, shut it, or we'll never find out what's going on." Kiki whisper-yelled.

"Follow me." Hannah started leading them away. Mera finally let go of Zoe. They all followed Hannah out of the alley and back to where the club entrance was.

"Wait over there." Hannah pointed to an area down the road away from the club. Zoe led them away and Hannah approached the bouncer. They watched as she spoke to him and then the bouncer ran off into the alley and Hannah joined her friends.

Zoe looked at their friends. "Can you guys trust us?" she asked.

"I can." Mera said, holding her hand up, which made Zoe smile.

Kiki and Jack both looked at Mera in shock, and she looked at them both and sighed. "I haven't had a friend except the two of you in forever. And they didn't hurt anyone who was *good*. Hannah probably saved that girl and us... not to mention Zoe." She gestured toward Zoe with a worried look. "I think that if we just hear them out, we'll understand."

Zoe and Hannah watched Kiki and Jack. It felt like a long time before Kiki's sigh broke the silence.

"All right, we'll hear you out." Kiki agreed, then looked at Jack who rolled his eyes and sighed.

"All right, fine. I agree with Kiki."

"Come on." Hannah waved her hand and she and Zoe led the group in silence all the way back to the mansion.

When they split away from the driveway and headed toward the cemetery, Hannah took the lead. Zoe fell back next to Mera, who put her arm around Zoe's shoulders. Zoe smiled at Mera, who was starting to feel more and more like another sister.

Hannah opened the black iron gate and walked through. Zoe and Mera followed with Kiki close behind. Jack groaned in disgust, but followed them through. They all followed Hannah through the cemetery, into the woods and to the clearing with the willow tree, the moonlight breaking through the trees like a beautiful painting.

"Wow." Mera marveled.

"It should be safe for us to talk here." Hannah told them.

Mera let go of Zoe and the five of them stood in a circle. Zoe next to Hannah, Kiki on Hannah's other side, with Jack between Kiki and Mera.

"Okay. Now please explain to me what the heck is going on." Kiki insisted.

"OK. Here's the full version…" Hannah sighed. "I am what is called a Protector. I have abilities that help me fight beings of evil, like what you saw tonight. The being that I killed wasn't human."

"What?" Kiki asked, disbelieving.

"We don't actually know everything about it. We just found out ourselves." Zoe came to Hannah's defense.

"What do you mean by not human?" Mera asked.

"Vampires, some werewolves, dark psyonics, things of that nature." Everyone but Zoe jumped at the voice.

Zoe and Hannah turned to see Jared. Zoe smiled at him.

"Oh." Mera sounded satisfied with their answer.

"Who are you?" Jack asked.

"This is Jared." Zoe answered him as Jared came over and stood behind them. She shifted so he could stand between them, as everyone looked back to her.

"What, I met him here." Zoe explained. She could see there were going to be questions later about that statement, but she let it go for the moment.

"Anyway, what Jared said." Hannah motioned toward Jared. "I'm not entirely sure what I'm supposed to do with this power, but I have it, so..."

Mera raised her hand.

"Yes, Mera." Hannah looked at her.

"What powers do you have? Telekinesis, empathy, stuff like that?"

"Mind reading?" Jack included.

"No. It's more stuff like super-strength, night vision,

heightened senses, super strong skin and super fast healing." Hannah explained.

"Oh. Okay." Kiki said.

Hannah looked up—obviously thinking deeply. "I'm trying to remember what the book said."

But Jared had already guessed at what she wanted to explain. "When a family has the protector gene, it can skip generations until it finds someone worthy and capable of handling the protector abilities and work that come with them."

Hannah shrugged dismissively. "That'd be me I guess." She said.

"I know this may seem unbelievable, unreal. But that vampire that we saw tonight *really did* turn to dust. This is real." Zoe turned to Jared. "Can you show them one more piece of evidence?"

He nodded and took a few steps back—and, as he leaned down his body changed from man to wolf, his clothes magically disappearing. Like he had told Zoe, he was a little bigger than the average wolf, but he was obviously a real wolf... not a werewolf.

Zoe squatted down near him. She looked Jared in eyes that were now yellow... not brown. She looked back and saw Kiki, Jack and Mera obviously shocked.

Hannah seemed to shrug it off. After all she had just dusted a vampire.

Zoe smiled and looked back at Jared. He walked over to her and she reached up and scratched behind his ears. He leaned his head against her fingers.

"H... H... Ho... How... How did he do that?" Kiki stuttered.

Zoe looked back, knowing that Hannah didn't know how to answer Kiki.. "He's a Shifter. Not a shapeshifter, he can't change into anything, he can only change into a wolf." she explained.

Jared took a step back and changed back into his human, clothed form. His eyes returned to their normal soft, brown color. He stood up and offered his hand to Zoe. She accepted it and he helped her stand.

"You can't really deny that." Hannah declared.

Jared and Zoe looked at each other, withholding any comments about how Hannah had done just that. They looked back at the group just as Mera, Jack and Kiki were exchanging glances.

Zoe's stomach tightened, worrying that they were about to lose three friends that they could've been close to.

Mera and Jack seemed to have an entire conversation with just their eyes. Then Mera rolled her eyes, looking away and sighing. Jack and Kiki did the same thing before Mera broke the silence.

"I believe." Mera paused. "And you don't have to worry about me spilling the secret and you don't have to worry about losing me as a friend." Saying this, she looked directly at Zoe.

Zoe could feel Jared's hard gaze on her back. Mera looked over at Kiki and gave her a wide-eyed look. Kiki turned to look at Hannah and Zoe.

"You don't have to worry about me spilling your secret either, or losing me as a friend." Kiki assured them, rolling her eyes again, but smiling.

A few seconds passed until Mera kicked Jack in the shin. He jumped back, exclaiming his pain.

"Ow! Yeah. Yeah. You don't have to worry about me either, we're all still friends. Although I'm rethinking things with Mera." Jack said in a joking tone, looking at Mera, who looked down to hide her laughter.

Zoe hid hers as well, but Kiki and Hannah didn't bother.

Zoe looked behind her to find Jared gone. She sighed. Hannah looked at Zoe, then glanced at where Jared had been standing.

Zoe could barely hear her, but under her breath Hannah whispered. "Goodbye."

Jack, Kiki and Mera walked Hannah and Zoe back to the house, then Jack escorted Mera and Kiki back to their house, after picking up a lone tree branch off the ground for protection.

Hannah and Zoe didn't say much to each other, they just walked upstairs together, went into their own rooms and prepared to go to bed.

ANOTHER CONFIDANT

After putting on her pajamas, Hannah sat on her bed. The realization that she had killed a man earlier that evening was just sinking in. Granted, he hadn't really been a man—and she had been protecting her sister and her friends at the time. And they believed in her.

But the fact remained... that she had killed something... that night. She'd killed some... thing last night as well. That was two vampires in two nights. Was this gonna be her life now? Killing vampires, monsters, and who knew what else?

She rubbed her hands together, like anyone else would. She didn't like the feeling that she'd killed—even if it was no longer really a person. She never wanted to do it again. She wondered if she could just knock the vampire out next time.

Then the thought hit her, what if someone didn't give her a chance? What if someone she cared about was in danger? What if she had no choice to kill again?

She had saved her sister, but then again that had been Zoe's plan all along, to get Hannah to accept herself by saving her sister. She was a genius, but she did have the advantage of knowing Hannah really well.

Hannah told herself that if anyone was in danger, she would try her best to incapacitate the vampire without killing them.

"I know that look." Hannah looked behind her at her balcony. She'd opened the doors when she came in.

Jared stood there, his arms crossed. He looked at Hannah, the white curtains waving in the wind in front of him.

"What look?" Hannah asked, standing to face him.

"I saw what you did tonight." Jared uncrossed his

arms and walked over in front of Hannah. He watched her.

"The fact that you have killed two vampires."

"Yes and?" Hannah asked, her face composed of a mask that she tended to put on in front of people she didn't know well.

"Killing vampires isn't always easy."

Hannah crossed her arms. "What's your point?"

"My point is that, you're probably thinking that you never want to kill another vampire in your life—and you can't think like that."

"What makes you think that you…"

"I just mean…" Jared interrupted Hannah. "I've seen this before, someone I knew once vowed to never again kill a vampire and it cost him."

Hannah flipped her hair off her shoulder. "What was your role in that story?"

Jared sighed. He seemed unsure about telling her. He looked away from her for a few seconds, then looked back into her eyes. "He was my father. When he married my mother, who was a Shifter, he didn't know about her secret, supernatural life. He found out when I was thirteen. That was when my powers began to show.

He helped her at first, but then he swore to never again kill anyone or anything. Not long after that, my sister and then my brother started showing abilities. My mother was fighting vampires in her cheetah form, when she got distracted by my father trying to knock out a vampire instead of killing it. She tried to save him but the vampire killed her first."

Jared paused, looking away. "My father was never the same after that. He was cold, distant, practically catatonic. I was fifteen. So believe me when I tell you, if you hesitate to kill a vampire, even once, they will know they can get the better of you and you *will* pay the price."

Hannah cleared her throat. "You're wrong. Not every situation is the same, I won't lose anyone I care about and I *won't* kill another vampire." Hannah knew she sounded naive. She probably would lose loved ones eventually, but she convinced herself that she could protect them and not kill vampires at the same time.

"I won't kill anyone, but I *will* protect my family." Hannah said, her tone stern and stubborn.

Jared turned around and headed toward the balcony. He looked down then back at Hannah. "Then they'll die."

Hannah looked up and then turned away, fiddling

with her fingernails.

"A heartbeat is all it takes, for one heartbeat you have everything, till one heartbeat later, when someone snatches it all away. It goes too fast. Try to remember that. Try."

When Hannah looked up, Jared was gone. Hannah rushed over outside her balcony, putting her hands on the rails. She saw a dark figure walking away toward the cemetery and then the dark figure disappeared into the trees.

Is he right? Am I wrong? Why me? I don't want to kill anyone —good or evil. Why now...

As the thoughts filled Hannah's head, a tear slipped down her cheek. She banged the rails once with her hands, then closed her eyes. A minute later, when she opened them, she lifted her hands and saw the marks on the rails.

It made her worry about what she could do to a person if she hit them too hard.

A TRUTH FROM THE PAST

Hannah was about to get into bed when she saw that her clock said 11:45 p.m.

"Hannah." A voice whispered.

"Amanda." Hannah went over to open her door, just in time to see Zoe about to knock. "You heard her?"

"Of course. Let's go!" Zoe said excitedly.

Hannah followed her sister out, closing the door

behind her. Zoe looked like she hadn't slept at all, but she was in her pajamas, and her hair was already in a braid.

"You know, we're gonna have to tell Amanda that this situation is affecting our sleep schedule." Hannah smiled. Zoe chuckled but didn't say anything.

They quickly tip-toed down the hall, around two corners, down another hall, then some stairs, around two more corners and down the hall around another corner then turned to face the basement door.

"Ready?" Hannah asked, taking Zoe's hand.

"Yep."

Hannah opened the basement door. No monsters were there. Hannah looked at Zoe, who nodded. Still holding Zoe's hand, she led her down the stairs.

When they reached the bottom, Hannah glanced at the entire, empty, concrete room before walking into the middle of the room and facing the spiderweb wall. "Amanda. We're here, where are you?" Hannah asked.

A minute passed before Amanda appeared. She seemed out of breath, which was strange for a ghost. She was almost frantic, hurried. "We don't have much time, we must hurry." Amanda said frantically, her eyes wide, Amanda looked to the left then the right, then to Hannah and Zoe.

"Okay, okay." Hannah motioned for her to calm down. "We found your grave buried in our graveyard, and we were wondering if you knew someone in our family?"

"And you died on the same day that our grandpa died, so we were wondering if there was a connection." Zoe asked.

"Oh no." Amanda said, looking up into the vast nothing. "I'm fading."

"What? Fading, what do you mean?" Hannah asked.

"The fading of my memory, I died long ago. And now my memory will fade away."

"But why? What do you mean?" Hannah asked.

"How long have you felt this way?" Zoe broke in.

"For two months." Amanda looked back at them.

"Grandpa." Hannah whispered.

"You were in love with Grandpa! Weren't you?" Zoe asked.

"Yes. We got married, but then when I died, Ray moved away because his pain was too great." Amanda explained, her expression turned tired and she started to look more and more transparent.

"Oh my goodness." Zoe said.

"Hannah, someone very dangerous is coming when I leave. Your grandfather was holding him back but now that he's gone you have to deal with him."

"What do you mean grandpa kept him here?" Zoe asked.

"That's not important, the point is that even though he is coming… someone worse is on their way now."

"Oh no!" Hannah exclaimed.

"What can we do to stop them?" Zoe asked her.

"Fight him, kill him, destroy him, I don't care, just…" Amanda paused, then her chest glowed.

"No, not yet, I didn't tell them anything yet." Amanda pleaded, looking up.

"What's going on?" Hannah asked, pushing Zoe behind her with her arm, but Zoe stayed at Hannah's side. She held onto Hannah's arm, but she didn't move.

"I'm moving on." Amanda said with tears in her eyes, a breeze blew in the basement from behind Hannah and Zoe.

"What do we have to do to get rid of him?" Hannah asked.

"His name is Paul." Amanda's voice was almost a whisper. "Trust yourself Zoe, and you'll know who to trust." Amanda paused and looked from Zoe to Hannah.

"Trust your sister and you'll be fine." Amanda said, then looked up. "Ray." Amanda smiled, then started floating up. "Goodbye girls." Then she disappeared along with the glow and breeze.

"Okay."

"Amanda!" Hannah hollered. "Amanda, don't leave us! We still have questions." Hannah curled her hands into tight fists.

"Next page in our story I guess." Zoe reached for her. "Let's go to bed."

"Yeah. Okay."

They slowly went back up the stairs, made their way back through the house—to their rooms... and went to bed.

MEMORY LANE

September 18th, 2018

As the sun was setting, Zoe sat in the backyard, in the grass at the edge of the drop off, with her legs dangling off the edge. She pondered the dream that she'd had recently. The green murky water, with seaweed flowing side to side, the claws wrapped around her ankle filled her memory. She'd looked down and the green eyes flashed in her mind.

Zoe opened her eyes and looked up, seeing her new backyard, complete with a lake. She crossed her arms, trying to keep them warm from the cool, fall breeze.

The weather had turned cooler since they'd first arrived. She wore brown leather boots, with low heels, black leggings and an orange sweater.

"Hey sis!" Hannah called to her, walking up to Zoe. "Sis?" Hannah bumped Zoe's shoulder.

Zoe looked up at Hannah. "Yeah?"

"You okay?" Hannah asked, sitting down next to Zoe and letting her legs dangle.

"Sorry, just deep in thought."

"Thinking about Amanda?" When she didn't answer, Hannah went on, "...or about Grandpa?"

"Just stuff."

"I thought you didn't like lakes."

"No. I like lakes just fine. It's just Lake Rikersfield that bothers me."

"Yeah. I get that."

"And I don't really get that drowning feeling a lot."

"You're having the nightmare again aren't you?"

It was a minute before Zoe answered her sister. "I was fine until Grandpa died. It was like he kept them away somehow."

"Yeah he did, didn't he? Why didn't you tell me you were having nightmares?"

"Because I'm not used to having you to talk to."

"Well you have me now, so get used to it." Hannah put her arm around Zoe's shoulders.

"Okay."

"Friends?"

"Better." Zoe looked at her. "Sisters."

"Family."

"By the way I should give this back to you." Zoe reached down her shirt and pulled out the necklace Hannah buried.

"I buried that."

"I know, I saw you and I went out later and dug it up."

"You." Hannah wagged her finger at Zoe.

"Ok. Well, if you don't want this..." Zoe started swinging the necklace back and forth in front of Hannah.

She grabbed the necklace and then pulled Zoe into a hug. "I love you, sis."

"I love you too. Do me a favor though and don't bury it again. Please. I'm not as strong as you. I've still got blisters."

Hannah sighed as she looked at the hills in the distance.

Zoe thought of the singing that she kept hearing.

Should I? Maybe I should tell her. Yeah, I'll tell her.

Now? Or later after we hang out with the gang?

Now, definitely now.

"Hannah." Zoe hoped Hannah wouldn't freak out.

"Yes?"

"Girls!" Martha called from the back door.

"Sorry." Hannah said to Zoe, who nodded understandingly.

"Yeah mom?" Hannah yelled back, looking back at the house.

"Your friends are here!" Martha yelled back.

"Coming!" Hannah yelled, then stood up and helped Zoe up. "What did you want to say?"

I can't tell her now, she would be tense, and wouldn't have fun, and she has enough to worry about with the Paul guy. I'll tell her later, when things calm down.

"Nothing, never mind." Zoe said. "Nothing important anyway. We can talk about it later"

Hannah shrugged as she reached up and put the necklace in place.

Hannah and Zoe met up with Kiki, Jack and Mera.

Zoe tried to put her worries out of her mind so that she could relax and wouldn't stress out her sister. For the second time, they went to the club. As soon as they got inside, Mera pulled them over to a booth. They all sat down but Zoe.

"I'm gonna go get a soda." Zoe yelled over the rock

song that the Diamonds were playing. Even as she was walking away from them, she felt like she had finally found her family, but something was missing, someone.

Amongst the singing, the loud drums, the people chatting here and there, Zoe heard something clearer than she hear anything else in that club, a little girl singing.

Zoe knew that what she was hearing wasn't actually in this room. She'd figured out a while ago that she was hearing the girl in something like her inner ear.

The singing started to quiet before the girl sang.

"Death."

Then the singing faded away as if it was never there. Zoe turned around, looking around for some evidence for what she'd just heard, seeing if anyone else had heard what she'd heard, but no one was reacting the way Zoe was. She was the only one looking around frantically, trying to make sure someone wasn't about to drop dead.

"Zoe, what's wrong?" Hannah asked, as she came up behind her.

Zoe froze... at least she felt like she was frozen... like she couldn't answer.

"Zoe?" Hannah asked, tapping Zoe's shoulder. She

was on the verge of panic... "Zoe?"

Zoe's eyes were wide, and she could feel something else in her life that was about to change.

Or else it already had.

THE RETURN

The night was everything like Paul remembered, cold, windy, dark. The wind blew against him, one of the small things he'd missed while being dead. He took in a deep breath, which was something else he had missed... feeling the cold autumn air in his lungs.

He looked up at the moon. It was more vibrant than he remembered. Or maybe being dead and coming back made everyone think life was more vibrant and crisp.

Paul's new minion, Dylan walked up next to him. He'd

been able to bring Dylan with him as well. He thought he might be valuable, given that the new protector has already killed him once. He might have some good insight. Although Paul mostly thought that he was an idiot and was only good as a halfway decent minion.

"Why'd you bring me back to life?" Dylan asked.

"Because, I need someone to watch people. Watch the Autumns. Help me." Paul said.

"So, I'm your slave?"

"No, you can live your life, I'll just need you to do a little of my dirty work." Paul was planning to fill Dylan's days with work.

"I can't do a lot of stuff in the day, I'm a vampire."

"I know, why do you think I had you meet me at night? I am not the moron here!" Paul said, leaning and looking at Dylan, wondering if he had picked the right idiot for his dirty work.

"I just figured that you were a creep." Dylan said, shrugging. "What do you want me to do with the Autumns?"

"Whatever you want, as long as you don't make direct contact."

"Are they dangerous?"

"Yes, but one is more dangerous than the other and you'll never see it coming." Paul and Dylan headed to the forest, into the dark of night...

where they disappeared.

ACKNOWLEDGEMENTS

I still remember when my mother and grandmother decided to participate in their first NaNoWriMo session. I was really too young to completely understand what they were doing—writing at the dining room table every evening after dinner while my brother and I played, watched a little television or just watched as they crafted story worlds out of thin air and imagination alone.

I also remember when I made the decision to follow in their footsteps. It wasn't easy. The first dozen stories I wrote were only a few pages. But, every story was a stepping stone to where I am today.

Thank you Mom, for encouraging me to help you write *The Alien's Daughter!* It changed so much about what I thought it meant to write a story.

Thank you Grams, for helping me with synonyms and descriptive words and phrases. And for putting up with me when I was completely ignoring you while I was immersed in my own story world.

Your encouragement, more than anything else, helped me to get here and I will be forever grateful!

And thank you to everyone who helped to inspire the characters and this story!

Q: What inspired you to write *Autumn Awakening?*

A: The inspiration actually came from a number of favorite television shows and books and movies. Mostly, when I was reading or watching, my imagination just sparked—and I would rush off to write about it.

Q: Is there something specific that led you to write this particular series?

A: The love of the characters. They're the type of characters who... you walk into their home, and you never want to leave.

Q: You mention that you followed in your mother and grandmother's footsteps... Do you think your writing style is more or less like theirs?

A: Not really. I feel like I have my own style. My own voice. I have definitely asked their advice at times, but the story flows the way my characters demand.

Q: Did you choose to write fantasy because it's what your mother writes? Or is there another reason?

A: I chose to write fantasy because it speaks to me. It had nothing to do with what other people write—or even what people favor to read. It just speaks to me.

Q: Is there another genre you are interested in writing —or that you would consider writing at some point in the future?

A: Fairy Tale retellings is one. I've actually already begun a story in what I hope will be a series. I am also interested in writing a futuristic fantasy series.

Q: Will there be more books in this series?

A: Heck yeah! I've already finished book two and sent it off for editing!

Q: Can we look forward to more books from you beyond this series?

A: Definitely! I hope to even branch out into young adult fiction someday.

Q: Who was your favorite character to write?

A: My favorite character to write was definitely Zoe. She constantly surprises me.

Q: Did you have a favorite part in this first book?

A: One of my favorite scenes in this first book is when Hannah finally accepts her gift and saves her sister, but my favorite part to write was when we were first introduced to Jared. I just knew he was going to be an interesting character.

Q: Do you have any advice for novice or debut authors—or for other young people like yourself who want to write?

A: Never let anything or anyone stand in your way! Use whatever you have at your disposal to write your story! I've used pencil and paper to write stories. I've used my tablet, my phone and my notebook computer to write! Getting them down in one form or another is what truly matters!

Never feel like you have to do what anyone else tells you to do—or what's "popular". Don't make yourself crazy trying to put in all of the elements that everyone wants. Write what your story needs!

In the four year process of writing my very first solo novel, I have had many people come up to me and tell me that I cannot do it. I cannot make it work. In my personal experience, the best thing to do in that situation is to block out the negative voices!

Surround yourself with the people who inspire you! Let those people be the ones who fuel and feed your storytelling!

About the Author

MACY Morrows is the youngest in three generations of authors. Like her grandmother and her mother, Macy followed her passion for the written word. She decided this at a very young age - and has been writing ever since.

Like her mother, JC, Macy prefers to inhabit the fantasy worlds she dreams up and put her own spin on beloved fairy tales, writing mainly for a middle grade audience

When Macy is not writing her fantastical tales, participating in author events and comic-cons, she can be found on

INSTAGRAM@MACYMORROWS
FACEBOOK@MACYMORROWS
GOODREADS@MACYMORROWS

FOR MORE INFO & BOOK NEWS, CHECK OUT HER WEBSITE: MACYMORROWS.WORDPRESS.COM

More by Macy Morrows

As if being a teenager isn't hard enough...

Can you imagine how it feels to wake up one day and find out that you are not who you thought you were?

If you're anything like me, you know it's hard enough trying to fit in—in high school—without having to deal with the knowledge that your dad is an alien part of the time. I don't even get how you can be an alien part of the time...

Not to mention all of the crazy new alien gifts you really wish you could return.

Oh well, at least I have an explanation for the blue hair.

So, not only do I get to deal with school bullies this fall, who I'm apparently not allowed to use my new abilities on, I have to keep anyone from finding out my secret... and keep my grades up.

Could life get any crazier!

As if I don't have enough to deal with...

It's crazy enough to find out, the hard way, that you are not who you thought you were.

But to have that kind of bombshell dropped on you, and then — to have your Dad ditch you — leaving you to figure stuff out all by yourself, with a Mom you can't tell anything about what's going on... and school enemies lurking around unexpected corners.

I mean... come on. It's summer!

Between trying to keep a tight grip on my sanity, not to mention my new crazy alien powers, dealing with Ashley and her band of terrible teens, not knowing if I still have a best friend or not is just the straw I do not need to be saddled with this summer.

Is it any wonder I feel like I just might lose it any second! And if I do... well, keeping the secret from Mom will be the least of my problems!

WELCOME TO SILVER CITY! Where Happily Ever After is still a modern girl's dream.

Meet Cindy, a soft-spoken maid in training who wishes she could do a little more than clean the Prince's toilets.

As good as orphaned, Cindy works for her step-mother, who owns a high class maid service that caters to the well-to-do families of Silver City.

Maree is not your average girl. She rides, climbs trees, is an expert archer, and a constant embarrassment to her very proper mother.

If only she could have been born a boy... like her three rambunctious younger brothers... who can do no wrong in their parents' eyes...

Chef. Genius. Chubby. Dork.

There are many words used to describe Rissa, chef-in-training, but for the most part she is too caught up in her cooking to pay much attention.

When push comes to shove, she doesn't let anything stop her, which is a good thing when it comes time to win the Silver City cooking contest.

COMING SOON

HIDDEN
legacy
what you don't know can change everything...
MACY MORROWS

About the Publisher

We here at
Mystic Moonstone Press
actively seek out fun and fantastical
stories that every member of the family
can read and enjoy!

We hope you will check out our works and
join us on our journey!